Margo's Café

Also by Tom Milton

Voices in Ramah
A Residue of Hope
Blind in Granada
A Contrite Heart
Milos and Amira
The Lost Summer
The Lineman
The Last Resort
The Godmother
Eden Valley
The Silver Locket
Orphans of War
Invisible Wounds
Leave of Absence
Outside the Gate
The Golden Door
Sara's Laughter
A Shower of Roses
Infamy
All the Flowers
The Admiral's Daughter
No Way to Peace

Margo's Café

Tom Milton

NEPPERHAN PRESS, LLC
YONKERS, NY

Published by Nepperhan Press, LLC
P.O. Box 1448, Yonkers, NY 10702
nepperhan@optonline.net
nepperhan.com

PUBLISHER'S NOTE
This is a work of fiction. Names, characters, places, and incidents
are the product of the author's imagination or are used fictitiously,
and any resemblance to actual persons, living or dead, events, or
locales is entirely coincidental.

Printed in the United States of America

Library of Congress Control Number: 2025932983

ISBN 978-1-7377413-9-8

Cover art was licensed from iStock Maria Tkach

For Marie

A good mother is a shield for her children
against many evils in life.
Aeschylus

Hastings-on-Hudson, 2024

ONE

MARGO WONDERED WHO he was and what he was doing at her café because unlike her typical customers he was wearing a suit, a gray suit with a white shirt and a red tie like politicians wore, so she was suspicious, but she wasn't at all prepared for what he did to her.

He came in after the rush of people doing takeouts on their way to work. He approached the counter where she was standing, and he ordered a small caffe latte and a plain croissant, which he paid for in cash, and then he sat at one of the tables.

While he took bites of his croissant and sips of his coffee he looked around as if he was seriously assessing the property. He was probably in his mid-thirties, the age of Margo's youngest daughter, Tricia. He had probably gone to college and majored in business and now worked for a company, or he wouldn't have been wearing a suit. She didn't know anything about suits because neither her father nor her husband had worn them to work, but she noticed that this young man's suit fit him perfectly, so it was probably expensive.

After he finished his breakfast he leaned back in his chair and called to her: "Are you Margo Walsh?"

"Yes," she said. "How can I help you?"

"Would you mind joining me?"

It sounded like a command rather than an invitation, and it made her wary. After a moment of hesitation she said: "Okay."

He watched her approach, and when she stopped and stood at his table he told her: "You may want to sit down."

At that point she realized that he was going to give her some bad news. While she remained standing he reached into his shirt pocket and took out a business card, which he offered her across the table.

The card said: "Richard Pierce, Vice President, RSC Investments, LLC." And it listed a New York City address.

"Okay," she said as calmly as possible. "What's this about?"

"It's about your lease."

It was a five-year lease which Margo had signed in 2019 without ever imagining that within nine months her business would be disrupted by covid. Her landlady was an elderly woman who out of the goodness of her heart had let her pay whatever rent she could during the time when restaurants were closed. She had died almost a year ago, and according to Margo's agent it was taking a while to settle the estate because of family conflicts.

"What about my lease?" she asked, looking directly into the man's cold gray eyes.

"It expires at the end of May," he said.

"I know, but I have an option to renew it."

"You do, at the market rent."

"Okay. So you want an increase of five percent?"

The man laughed mirthlessly. "That's not the market rent. The market rent is double what you're paying now."

"Double? You're crazy. You could never rent this place for that much."

"We could, and we will."

She was still standing, but she felt as if she had been hit by something, and she steadied herself by grasping the back of a chair. She looked again at the business card, saying: "RSC Investments. Who are you?"

"We're the new owner of this building. We bought it from the estate," he added.

"And you're based in the city?"

He nodded. "Yes."

"Well, you don't know the market here. If you look around, you'll see that there are five empty stores in this village."

"But they're not prime locations like this."

"You think this is a prime location? I'm the fourth business to occupy this space in the past ten years."

"That only means they weren't good businesses."

"How can you say that? You don't know what they were."

"I have a record of every tenant that's occupied this space from when the building was constructed ninety years ago."

She glared at him, disliking him for several reasons, including for being a know-it-all. "Well, I have a good business here, but I couldn't pay double what I'm paying now. I could only pay a five percent increase."

"It's not negotiable," he said, pushing back his chair.

"Then you'll hear from my lawyer," she said, doubting it would deter him.

"Your lawyer can't do anything about it. Your lease only gives you an option to renew at the market rent. And the market rent is whatever we say it is," he said, standing up.

She noticed that he was shorter than the average man and he had a small, thin mouth. She could see how women might have rejected him, engendering a need to get back at them. She felt like saying: "We'll see about that," but conscious of it being a standard retort in a playground quarrel she only repeated: "You'll hear from my lawyer."

"Fine," he said. Before leaving he reached into his pants pocket and left a handful of change on the table.

"Asshole," she muttered. Since there were no customers who needed attention she sat down at the table and fully confronted her situation. She was seventy years old, and she depended on her income from this business to help pay the property taxes on the house in which she had raised her family and still lived with her middle daughter, Lindsey, and a granddaughter, Keira. Her only other sources of income were Social Security, the individual retirement accounts which she and her husband had put their meager savings into, and Lindsey's contributions which paid for the utilities. Those sources covered her basic needs, but without the income from the café she wouldn't be able to stay in her house. Of course she could sell it, but the proceeds of the sale would be divided equally between her and her two remaining siblings, so it wouldn't leave her enough money to buy or rent an apartment with the space she needed for her family in an area where she had lived her whole life.

She could try to get a job. She had worked more than twenty years for a real estate firm in the village, but that ended when the owner retired and wound down the business, and then she had worked for almost ten years at a doctor's office, but that ended when he merged his practice into a group that used a complex computer system for processing claims. She struggled to learn the new system, but it defied her, and by then she really hated the job, so with the encouragement of her family and friends she started a business where she could apply her people skills. So she did have a useful set of skills, but at her age who would hire her?

At that moment she caught a glimpse of Chavo through the kitchen door, and she realized that she had been thinking only of herself and not of Chavo, the young man who worked for her from eight to three, making breakfast and lunch. It was his second job, his main job being from four to ten at an Italian restaurant in Irvington. Like most of the people working in kitchens he was an immigrant, but since he was only a child of five when his parents illegally brought him here from Mexico he had a special status in which he might have a chance of becoming legal someday and was temporarily not at risk of being deported. Now he was in his late twenties, married to a young woman with the same status who had delivered a baby boy about three months ago. They lived in an apartment in South Yonkers which they could afford because of Chavo's second job. So if Margo closed the café he would have to find another job, which might not be easy because restaurants still hadn't fully recovered from covid.

Concerned for him, she shifted her focus from the problem of paying the taxes on her house to the problem of paying the increase in the rent for the café, which led her to wonder how she could increase the income from her business. In theory she could increase that income by extending her hours of operation, but that would mean having a full-time restaurant, and from what she heard from the owners of the other restaurants in the village few of them were doing well, and they would have agreed that the last thing the village needed was another restaurant. With her café she had found a niche in the market because only one of the restaurants was open for breakfast and only a few were open for lunch. But even if there was a need for another restaurant, she couldn't be here after three because she had to be at the house when Keira, who had just turned twelve, got home from school. And there was simply no question of leaving Keira alone in the house. So if she wanted to extend her hours of operation she would have to find a partner, someone willing to invest and work in a business that was so risky that no bank would lend to it. And where would she find such a partner?

By now it was time for her regular customers to start appearing. They were mostly single women around her age who lived in nearby apartments, so they could walk here. The other people who came here for breakfast were men and women who worked at home, as more of them did now than before covid. The people in the latter group would use their phones to check messages and catch up on the news, and unlike the older customers they would rarely talk with each other.

Today her first customer was Flora, a gentile woman who lived in an apartment on Maple Avenue and was in her early eighties. Her husband had died about ten years ago but had left her a comfortable pension from his career as a banker in the city. Flora usually ordered poached eggs, bacon, and white toast with the peach jam that Margo made.

"Good morning, Flora," Margo greeted her. "How are you doing?"

"I'm doing just fine," Flora said, smiling. "How are you?"

"I'm fine," she lied, putting up a brave front. She led Flora to the table in the corner where she always sat. "Would you like some coffee?"

"Yes, please. I'm only half awake."

"Yeah, I know the feeling. What would you like to have for breakfast?"

"I'll have the usual. I'm a creature of habit."

"There's nothing wrong with that. As my mother used to say, habits keep us from getting into trouble."

Flora laughed. "I don't know what kind of trouble I could get into now."

"Oh, you'd be surprised."

Flora nodded, smiling speculatively.

Margo went into the kitchen, where she found Chavo at the stove stirring a pot of soup. With a colorful kerchief around his head he looked like a kid playing pirate.

"Mm, that smells good," she told him. "What is it?"

"It's pozole," he said. "You want to taste it?"

"Yeah, sure." Since he had learned his trade in Italian kitchens he usually stuck with that cuisine for the items on his menu, but every now and then he drew from what he had learned from his mother.

He found a spoon and dipped it into the pot and after waving it back and forth to cool the soup he offered it to her.

Tasting it, she liked it. "That's great. You should make this more often."

"*Gracias*," he said, inclining his head to her.

It made her determined to save his job.

After giving him the order from Flora she went back out and greeted another elderly woman, a regular customer who came here for breakfast. She was a sturdy woman in her late seventies with pink cheeks and pure white hair. Her name was Sally, and she lived in the same building as Flora. She greeted Flora and as usual went to her own table. They would eat their breakfasts separately and then get together at the same table where they had another cup of coffee and talked about their children and grandchildren.

Margo went to Sally, and after exchanging some words with her about the weather, which in late February was acting more like early April, she took the order. Sally was having a cheese omelet with multi-grain toast and butter.

Within a half hour all but two of the tables were occupied, mostly with solos but three of them with deuces, including a man and woman in their twenties who lived together above the antique store on the corner. They had hybrid jobs, so they worked at home a few days a week, usually on the same days, and Margo could tell from their body language that while they were at home together they weren't always working.

Since her customers were taken care of she made some phone calls to her suppliers, beginning with the bakery in the Bronx where she got croissants, rolls, and bread. The croissants, which her customers said were the best in the River Villages, were a major draw to her café. She called her supplier of dairy products and then her supplier of chicken and meat. She was on the phone with her supplier of coffee when her friend Greta arrived for lunch.

Greta was a petite woman who lived in one of the old three-story apartment buildings south of the bridge. Greta had grown up in that building, and she was the same age as Margo, so they had met in kindergarten and gone through elementary school together at St. Matthew and then to the public high school. Upon graduating they didn't go to college, they took courses at a business school in White Plains where Margo learned how to be a secretary and Greta learned how to be a bookkeeper. While Margo worked for the real estate firm in Hastings her friend worked for a large construction company in Yonkers, where she met the man she would marry. Greta lived in Yonkers on her own for a while and then returned to her family home in Hastings, where she raised her two children. She lost her husband five years ago but her children still lived in the area. Her son had a job with good pay, good hours, and good benefits driving a truck for the village's Department of Public Works, and her daughter was a pre-school teacher in Yonkers. Like Margo she had three grandchildren, and like Margo she went to the eleven-thirty Mass at St. Matthew. So the two of them had a lot in common.

As usual they greeted each other with a hug, and Margo led Greta to a table in the corner that she had saved for her. After getting settled at the table Greta told her: "You don't look good."

"I don't feel good," Margo admitted. "Something happened. When I have a chance I'll tell you about it."

"Is it your health?"

"No, thank God. It's my business."

Greta nodded. "Well, I can stay here as long as you want. So what's the soup for today?"

"We have minestrone, but Chavo also made pozole. It's a Mexican soup with white corn. I tasted it, and I liked it."

"Mm. Is it spicy?"

"No. I mean, it has a little heat, but just enough to bring out the flavors." She knew that when Greta cooked at home she often added hot pepper flakes to bring out the flavors.

"Okay. I'll try it. And I'll have a wedge with ham, provolone, and lettuce."

"With oil and vinegar?"

"Oh, yeah. You know I don't like mayonnaise."

She took the order to the kitchen and returned with a cup of pozole. She would have brought a bowl if it had been minestrone, which she knew Greta liked.

After setting the cup on a saucer in front of her friend she waited.

Greta dipped her spoon into the cup and gently blew over the liquid and finally slurped the soup into her mouth. She had an expression on her face like someone tasting wine.

"Well?"

"I like it," Greta proclaimed. "It has just the right amount of heat."

"I'll tell Chavo."

"Yeah, he knows how picky I am."

When she went into the kitchen to get the wedge she told Chavo that Greta had liked the pozole.

"*Gracias*," he said, inclining his head as if a reviewer had given him a five-star rating.

For the next hour or so Margo was busy attending customers. Some of the people who came for lunch took prepared food home for dinner, which they could heat up in a toaster oven or a microwave. Today the choices were chicken parmesan and veal with artichokes, and since Chavo varied the prepared food during the week it was possible to have a different meal every day, which met the needs of elderly people living alone. If Margo hadn't had Lindsey and Keira to feed, she would have taken advantage of the service because she knew from experience how hard it was to cook only for yourself.

It was after two when things slowed down enough for her to join Greta. She brought two coffees and sat in the chair opposite her friend, who had been alone for more than an hour but unlike the younger people didn't need a phone for company.

"So what happened?" Greta asked her.

"They're doubling my rent."

"They? Who are they?"

"A company that bought this building from my landlady."

"Do you know anything about them?"

"No, except that they're assholes."

Greta took a sip of coffee and asked: "Does this company have a name?"

"Yeah." She found the card in the pocket of her jeans and handed it to Greta.

"RSC Investments? They're probably a front for black money."

"Black money? What do you mean?"

"Money from criminal activities—like drug dealing, human trafficking, and arms trading."

"But why would they buy this building?"

"That's how they launder their ill-gotten gains. They buy real estate, and they use fronts like this company so the government can't trace it."

"But why here?"

"They've been buying real estate in the city for years, so maybe they've run out of things to buy there. And it's less conspicuous to buy something here than in the city."

After thinking for a moment Margo said: "If we could find out who they are, then maybe we could stop them."

"You'll never find out who they are," Greta told her, shaking her head. "They're hidden under layers of shell corporations."

"So what can I do?"

"Well, isn't there a law that limits how much they can raise your rent?"

"I don't know. There were limits during covid, but the guy said the market rent is whatever they say it is."

"He's probably right, but check with your lawyer just to make sure."

"Okay." She made a mental note to check with Robert, the local lawyer who had served her family for many years, and then she said: "You know our income and expenses, so you know what would happen to this business if they doubled the rent."

"Yeah. It wouldn't survive," Greta said.

"But I need the income from this business to help pay the property taxes on my house."

"Well, there are other possible sources of income."

"You mean like getting a job."

"Yeah. You have skills."

"I have people skills, but I don't have skills like you have." Greta still made money by providing bookkeeping services to local businesses, including the café. "And I don't know if there's a demand for the skills I have."

"There must be a demand for real live people in customer service. People don't want to talk with Indians or robots. So maybe you could work for a call center."

"Yeah, maybe. But according to a woman I met at Tierney's who works at home for a call center, the pay sucks, so it probably wouldn't be enough."

Greta was silent, and then she said: "It's not right that people our age can't afford to live in their homes because of the high property taxes."

"Oh, I agree. The taxes are too high, and they keep going up."

"They keep going up because people from the city with a lot of money are bidding up the prices of homes in our village and increasing the assessments."

"Like the people across the street from me. They paid two million dollars for their house, and it wasn't worth even half that much."

"Thank God my landlord hasn't sold his buildings. And he always treats us well because he values his tenants."

"You still have rent control, don't you?"

"Yeah. I have a three-year lease with a limit on the increase in my rent. But I don't mind paying an increase to cover inflation."

"I don't either," Margo said, having expected a five-percent increase.

After a moment Greta asked: "Have you considered selling your house?"

"Yeah, I have. But where would I live? I'd need an apartment with three bedrooms, and how much rent would I have to pay?"

"For anything in a good neighborhood you'd have to pay four to five thousand a month."

"That's what I figured. And that would eat up my money from the sale in a few years."

"How do you figure?"

"I'd have to share the proceeds with my siblings."

"Oh, I forgot. You have an agreement with them that you can live in the house, but if you sell it you have to share the proceeds with them."

"That's our agreement. And I think it's fair."

Greta took a sip of coffee. "As a senior citizen don't you get a reduction in your property taxes?"

"Yeah, but it doesn't help much. I still have to pay more than Lindsey earns from her job at the hospital."

"I guess that explains why young people aren't buying houses."

"Or renting apartments. There's no way Lindsey could pay the rent for two bedrooms. Or even one bedroom."

"Okay. So you should try to keep this business."

"That's what I think. But I'd have to increase my income from it. And the only way would be to expand the hours of operation."

"You mean by doing dinner?"

"Yeah. But I'd need a partner to be here in the evening. I have to be at the house when Keira gets home from school."

"When does she get home from school?"

"Around three-thirty."

"When does her mother get home from work?"

"Around five, depending on the traffic."

"Keira can't be at home alone for an hour and a half?"

"No, she can't. And you know why."

"Yeah," Greta sighed.

"In any case, if I did dinner without a partner I'd have to be here from eight in the morning until ten at night, and I don't think I could work that many hours."

"What about Chavo?"

"He might do it, I mean if I paid him what he makes at his other job. But if he was working in the kitchen he couldn't manage the front."

"Okay. So you'd need a partner."

"But even if I found a partner I could trust, I don't know if there's a market in this village for another restaurant. We already have nine restaurants."

"We have that many?"

"Yeah, we do. Plus five takeout places."

Greta moved her fingers as if she was counting to verify those numbers, and then she said: "Then your restaurant would have to offer something we don't have now."

"Well, we have two Italian restaurants, a French restaurant, a seafood place, a gastropub, a sushi place, a Chinese—"

"The Chinese is only takeout."

"But people who want Chinese go there."

"What about Greek?"

"We have a diner."

"I mean upscale Greek."

"There's one in Irvington."

"What about Spanish?"

"People don't know what Spanish is. They think it's the same as Mexican."

"Then what about Mexican?" Greta said.

"Someone tried that, remember? Where the seafood place is now. And it didn't succeed."

"They didn't have Chavo as a cook. You know, I really liked that pozole. So maybe you could do upscale Mexican."

"There's one in Irvington."

"Does Irvington have all the upscale restaurants?"

"They have most of them. They have a lot of money there."

"We have a lot of money here—from all those people who move here from the city and pay too much for houses."

Margo considered. "Well, it doesn't look like selling my house or getting a job will go very far in solving the problem, so it looks like my best option is increasing the income from my business."

"I agree. So I'll think about where I'd want to go if I went out for dinner."

They got up from the table and went to the counter, where Greta settled her account, and then Margo went into the kitchen, where Chavo was cleaning up. For a moment she watched him, marveling at the scrupulous way he scoured the grill, and she could imagine him as a partner. So after a moment of hesitation she asked: "Do you think we could have a successful Mexican restaurant here?"

"Here?" he said, looking at her blankly.

"Yeah, here. For dinner."

He frowned. "Well, I don't know if there's a market for a Mexican restaurant here. Wasn't there one that failed?"

"There was, but it wasn't upscale."

"There's an upscale Mexican restaurant in Irvington. I worked there for a while. They had a few unusual dishes, but people mostly ordered tacos and enchiladas. Anyway, I'd rather work in an Italian restaurant. It's a much better business."

"Okay. I just wondered. How are Lupe and Pablo?"

"They're fine," he said, smiling. He dug into the pocket of his pants and pulled out his phone. He scrolled through a lot of pictures and then showed her a recent one of Pablo, who had big dark eyes.

"He's adorable," Margot said.

"He's only three months, but he's very active, and he sure knows how to get our attention."

"God bless him."

She left the kitchen and went to the counter, where she added up the chits for the day. It had been a good day, but even if every day was as good as this one she wouldn't have enough income to pay a doubled rent.

After flipping the CLOSED sign on the door she cleaned the tables and straightened the chairs. She mopped the floor, and she put things away, and she waited for Chavo to leave before she locked up. For a while she stood on the sidewalk facing the window of her café and remembering how she had survived during covid. By distributing fliers and posting announcements on the internet she had let people know that her business would remain open, that customers could order by phone or by email, and that they could pick up their food at a table on the sidewalk in front of the café. She had also done deliveries within the village, having asked customers to give her their addresses. Keira, whose classes had been moved to the internet where like most children her age she had trouble learning, was eager to get out of the house and do something helpful, so she had done the deliveries within walking distance of the café. The business had done well enough so that Margo could pay her landlady the full rent and still have enough money to help pay her property taxes.

Bolstered by the memory of how her business had survived covid, she was determined to survive the present threat. As she gazed into the window of her café she imagined what she could do here with the right partner. And then she turned and started walking home.

It wasn't as cold as usual for this time of year but there was still a chill in the air, and she zipped her coat up to her throat to hold in her bodily warmth.

TWO

SHE LIVED ABOUT a half mile from her café, and she walked on Warburton to Broadway, where she waited for the traffic light to cross the busy street, and then she went onto her street, which was one block long, dead ending at the raised path of the Old Croton Aqueduct. There were seven houses on her side of the street, including the modest houses built in the early 1900s for families of men with mid-level jobs at the factories on the riverfront. They were similar but not identical, and they all had front porches. A few of them still had the asbestos shingles that were installed during the 1930s, covering the original clapboard, but people who had bought these houses since the 1980s had removed the shingles, revealing clapboard that had been protected by the shingles all those years. Due to fire regulations parking was allowed on only one side of the street, and since not all the houses had driveways the available spaces were usually filled.

Her house was the fourth house from Broadway, so they didn't hear the traffic, and the fourth house from the aqueduct path, so they didn't get the litter. Her father bought it in 1956 for less than people now paid for a car, though it was a lot of money at the time. He had a job at Anaconda Wire & Cable, the largest factory on the riverfront, which employed more than two thousand people on three shifts. He was paid enough so that he could afford to move his family from an apartment in Yonkers to a house in Hastings with four bedrooms. The move was precipitated by the birth of their second child, Colleen, and its timing was good because two years later they had a third child, Audrey, so by then they needed at least three bedrooms. Two years later when they had a fourth child, Patrick, they definitely needed all four bedrooms. As the eldest Margo had her own bedroom, and as the only boy Patrick had his own bedroom while Colleen and Audrey shared a bedroom. Neither of them was happy about sharing a bedroom, and as soon as they could they left home and lived in their own places, Colleen in the city and Audrey across the river in West Nyack.

It was five steps up to the porch, which Margo climbed with a hand on the railing. On stairs she always held on to a railing because from her experience with people her age or older she knew what could happen if she fell, and she couldn't afford to let that happen. She stopped and opened the mailbox and took out the mail and unlocked the front door and let herself into the front hall. The stairs were on the left and the living room was on the right, an arrangement that someone told her was Victorian, but she knew nothing about architecture, she only knew what she liked, and she liked having the stairs on the left and not in the middle like in some houses. She went from the hall through the living room and through the dining room and into the kitchen, where she set the mail on the counter. It didn't take her long to sort through the mail, which included catalogs, an offer to replace the windows in her house, an appeal from Catholic Charities, and the Con Ed bill. There were no personal letters because with email and text messages no one wrote letters any more.

The clock on the counter told her it was almost three-thirty, so she sat down and waited for Keira, who would be home shortly. Keira was in seventh grade, and she had only a short walk home from school. She usually went to Five Corners, where she then headed north on Broadway. She had a friend who lived nearby who once talked her into walking home on the aqueduct path, but Margo told her not to do that again even in the company of another girl because there had been some incidents on the path, and as far as Margo knew, Keira hadn't done that again.

But she had other worries about her granddaughter, who was at the awkward age of early adolescence and had some mental health issues, including depression and ADHD. When Keira was nine her mother, following the advice of a pill-pushing shrink, had put her on a drug for depression which not only didn't help the poor girl but also made her condition worse, so after some fierce arguments between Margo and her daughter, and with the guidance of a more competent doctor, Keira had gradually stopped taking the drug for depression, though she continued taking the drug for ADHD, along with many other children at the school. Having seen evidence of Keira's inability to concentrate, Margo didn't argue against this drug, but she believed that the problem could be treated more effectively by getting children to spend less time on social media. She refused to accept the contention by some analysts that children were not anxious and depressed because they spent so much time on social media, they spent so much time on social media because they were already anxious and depressed. It was a clever argument but it didn't explain why so many children were anxious and depressed.

When she had reminded Greta of why she couldn't leave Keira home alone she was referring to things that the girl had done while under the influence of social media. A few months ago Keira, who for some reason had been let out early from school and had gotten home before Margo, attempted to pierce her nose with the sharp point of the nail scissors, presumably egged on by someone on social media who made her feel like a loser for not having any piercings. A few weeks earlier Keira had asked her mother to take her to a place where she could get her nose pierced by a professional, but Lindsey had said no, and Margo supported her, reminding Keira that her body was a temple of the Holy Spirit, so she should not disfigure it. Unable to stop the bleeding of the ugly wound that Keira inflicted on herself, Margo drove her immediately to their family practitioner, who disinfected the wound and stitched it. The girl was lucky it didn't leave much of a scar.

"Hey, I'm home," she heard Keira call from the front hall.

"I'm in the kitchen," she called back.

There was a thud from Keira dropping her backpack, and then the girl appeared in the doorway. She had reddish blond hair tied back in a ponytail, spacy blue eyes, and fair skin, dotted with tiny red spots that she tried to hide with makeup.

"Are there any cookies left?" she asked, advancing into the kitchen. She was a bit thin, below the normal weight for her body, but at least she didn't have eating disorders. She just didn't like food unless there was a treat like the peanut butter cookies that Margo made.

"I think so," Margo said. They kept the cookies in a tin whose place was on the last of the four counter chairs, where usually no one sat. Except for special occasions they had their meals at the counter, the three of them with Keira in the middle between her mother and her grandmother.

Keira lifted the tin from the chair and pried it open and took out two cookies, and then she sat down on her usual chair and took a dainty bite of a cookie. She didn't drink milk with cookies because she was severely lactose intolerant, a condition that ran in the family.

"So how was school?" Margo asked her.

"Eh," the girl said, munching. "The usual shit."

"Was it your teacher?"

"No, she wasn't the problem."

"What was the problem?"

"Oh, you know. The snotty rich kids talking about what they're going to do this summer."

"Most of the kids aren't snotty, are they?"

"No, most of them are nice, but it only takes a few of them to—"

She waited for Keira to complete the thought, but when she didn't Margo asked: "To do what?"

"To make me feel like a loser."

"Oh, come on. They can't make you feel anything. You choose how you feel."

"You always say that, but it's not easy."

"I know it's not easy," Margo agreed. "Nothing is easy. You just have to remind yourself that your mother loves you, your grandmother loves you, and God loves you, so no one can make you feel like a loser."

"Yeah, I know," Keira said as if she didn't know.

"Well, what are these snotty rich kids going to do this summer?"

Keira took another bite of cookie and chewed for a while. "They're going to the Hamptons, they're going to Cape Cod, they're going to Spain. They're going everywhere."

"Are they going to New Jersey."

"None of them mentioned New Jersey. What's there?"

"A lot of things. But people from this village who aren't rich go to New Jersey for the beaches."

"I remember going to a beach before covid. Was that in New Jersey?"

"No, it was in Connecticut." She had rented a place for a week in Milford, which was only an hour and half away. Within the past three months Lindsey had split with her husband, Jack had died, and she had given up trying to learn that computer system for processing claims, so she splurged to help her family through a difficult time.

"Could we go there again?"

"Maybe," she said, not knowing where she would get the money.

"If we do, then I'll be going somewhere."

"Well, in the meantime don't let those snotty rich kids get you down. You're a gift from God, you're the best thing that ever happened to your mother and me. So keep that in mind."

"I will," Keira said, though it didn't sound like a commitment.

"Would you like to play checkers?" They played this game every day after Keira got home from school. It was a way to keep the girl from getting on her phone and being lured into the trap of social media. Of course the phone had been an issue from day one because Lindsey refused to deal with it, so Margo had to ban it from meals and take it away from Keira at bedtime so she wouldn't stay up all night enthralled by its screen.

"Sure. I'll get it." Keira got up and went into the dining room and got the game out of the cabinet where they kept it. She returned to the kitchen and set the board on the counter in front of them. They weren't sitting opposite each other because the counter was rounded, but they were used to playing at angles to the board.

"Who gets black today?" Margo asked.

"I think you do," Keira said, though that might not have been the case. Among her many virtues, Keira was generous.

"Okay." The player with black got the first move, which might have given an advantage to players at a higher level, but at their level Margo didn't think it made any difference.

They set their pieces in the starting position, and then Margo made the first move, which Keira countered without hesitation. They had played so many times that their initial moves were routine. But as soon as one of them deviated from a pattern things got interesting.

Margo had learned from their games of checkers that Keira had a high level of intelligence and a keen sense of strategy. It was something that only one of Keira's teachers had seen in her while the others seemed to accept her low performance at the usual learning activities as indicative of her potential. Of course, Margo had to admit that when Keira wasn't interested in something it completely failed to hold her attention, and her mind wandered, only God knew where. At times while they were sitting at the counter before playing checkers Margo noticed that Keira's mind was somewhere else, and she asked her what she was thinking about, but Keira said nothing, not as if she was evading the question but as if she was honestly answering it. In the middle of the night when she couldn't get back to sleep after getting up to pee Margo tried thinking about nothing, but she was unable to. So if Keira really did think about nothing she had an ability that Margo didn't have, and that might be a blessing for her.

Keira won the first game, Margo won the second, and they were playing a third game when Lindsey got home, looking wiped out. She worked as a mental health worker at a private hospital that treated children with serious psychiatric issues. Of the three daughters Lindsey always got the best grades in school, and she successfully completed a bachelor's degree in psychology from St. Catherine College and was working on a master's degree when she dropped out after a breakup with a boyfriend. When she took her present job she still intended to resume working on her master's degree, for which the hospital provided tuition assistance, but then she met Brandon, she got pregnant, and she had to get married. The marriage lasted almost six years, but after enduring his drug addictions and repeated infidelities Lindsey finally got a divorce, and now at the age of thirty-six she no longer even pretended she would get a master's degree, so she was stuck in a low-paying job, working the day shift from eight to four, though that was an improvement over her schedules before she had seniority.

Upon entering the kitchen Lindsey put an arm around Keira's shoulder and gave her a kiss, and then she went to the refrigerator, opened the door, and took out a bottle of wine, the pinot grigio they usually drank. Margo didn't ask about her day because it almost never went well.

"Would you like some wine?" she asked Margo.

"Yeah, sure. It's after five."

"Who said we have to wait until five to have a drink?"

"I don't know. My parents waited until five."

The bottle of wine had already been opened, so Lindsey only had to get two glasses from the cupboard over the sink and pour some wine into them. "Did they really wait until five?"

"Usually. Though when my father jumped the gun he'd say it was five somewhere in the world."

Uninterested in their conversation Keira started taking her phone out of the pocket of her jeans.

"You can play on your phone after we have dinner," Margo told her, "but not now."

Keira sighed, but she obeyed her grandmother.

Lindsey handed a glass of wine to Margo and went around the counter and sat in her usual chair. She had inherited dark hair and dark eyes from Margo's mother, and most of the time she had a somber face, as she did now. It struck Margo that it was a long time since she had seen her daughter happy.

As a way of joining the adults in conversation Keira said: "Gramma said we can go to the beach this summer."

"I said maybe," Margo said.

"But all the kids in my class are going somewhere this summer."

"I thought it was only the snotty rich kids."

"It's not only them."

"Where would we go?" Lindsey asked.

"Where we went several years ago."

"Well, I could take a vacation in August."

"And I could close the café for a week. But I don't know if I have the money." Margo stopped there, not yet ready to tell them she might no longer have a business in August.

"I could help pay for it," Lindsey said.

"Then maybe we can do it," Margo said cautiously.

"Can we go where we went before?" Keira asked, evidently having some good memories of their week in Milford.

"Yeah, if it's available. I'll check and see. What week in August?" she asked Lindsey.

"I don't know. I guess the first or the second week."

"Okay," Margo said. She sipped the wine, wondering how much it would cost now to rent that place for a week.

After finishing her glass of wine Lindsey got up, saying: "I'm going to change. So what's for dinner?"

"Chicken cacciatore and pasta."

"That sounds good. I'll be right back."

Lindsey was a challenge to cook for because there were so many things she wouldn't eat, including beef and pork and shellfish, so they had chicken frequently. Margo had a lot of recipes for chicken, most of them in cookbooks that she kept in a cabinet beyond the stove which had windowed doors, like all the upper cabinets in her kitchen so she could see what was in them. Also, there were several three-ring binders on the far side of the counter with recipes that she had collected from cooking magazines and from the internet.

Tonight she was making a chicken dish she had learned from her mother, who made everything from scratch, though she might have approved of the canned San Marzano tomatoes that Margo was using instead of fresh tomatoes. She wouldn't have approved of the skinless, boneless chicken breasts that Margo was using instead of a whole chicken cut up into pieces. But her mother didn't have to deal with such picky eaters. Back then, you ate whatever your mother prepared, and if you didn't you went hungry.

She chopped an onion and started cooking it in extra light olive oil while she skinned two large cloves of garlic and minced them. When the onion was translucent she added the garlic and cooked it for about two minutes before adding half of her glass of white wine. She spooned the tomatoes onto her cutting board and sliced them into small pieces and scraped them from the board into the pan with a pinch of dried basil and let them cook over medium heat while she salted and peppered the chicken breasts.

By the time Lindsey returned in the loose-fitting pants and top she wore at home Margo had a pot of water boiling for the pasta. In a fresh pan she browned the chicken breasts in oil and then added them to the pan with the sauce and cooked them. Meanwhile she dropped a pound of spaghetti into the boiling water and stirred it with a metal pasta fork, a replacement for the plastic one that had lost a tooth. When the pasta was almost al dente she transferred it to the pan with the sauce and chicken, and she stirred it until it was done. She served it in bowls which Keira had helpfully placed on the counter, and they sat down to eat.

"I got a call from Tricia last night," Lindsey said.

"You did?" Tricia was the youngest of Margo's three daughters. She completed one semester at St. Catherine but dropped out early in her second semester and got a job as a waitress at an Irish pub in Dobbs Ferry. After learning how to mix drinks she got a job as a bartender at the same pub, and she continued working as a bartender, changing jobs about every six months and changing boyfriends just as often. She worked long enough to save money for a trip, she quit her job, she went on the trip with her boyfriend, and after the trip she broke up with her boyfriend. It was as if her only purpose of having a job was to save money for a trip, and her only purpose of having a boyfriend was to go on a trip with him. "What's happening with her?"

"She quit her job, and she's going to Mexico with her boyfriend."

"Is he paying for it?"

"He's paying for half of it."

"He should pay for all of it. I mean, if he's as rich as he pretends to be."

"He offered to pay for all of it," Lindsey said, "but she wouldn't let him. She doesn't want to be dependent on him."

"What's in Mexico?" Keira asked.

"Mariachis," Lindsey said.

"What's a mariachi?"

"It's a band of musicians who play happy music."

"Are they happy?"

"Mm, I don't know. I guess they're happy when they play that music."

"So the music makes them happy?"

"I guess. Does music make you happy?"

"If I like the music, it does," Keira said. "But I don't like all kinds of music."

"I don't either," Lindsey said. Then after a silence she reminded Margo: "She went to New Orleans only about six months ago with her previous boyfriend."

"The retired cop," Margo recalled.

"What's in New Orleans?" Keira asked.

"Restaurants and bars," Lindsey said, though she had only heard about New Orleans, she had never been there.

"We have restaurants and bars here, so why go there?"

"The restaurants and bars there are different."

"How are they different?"

"The restaurants serve spicy foods," Margo said, based on what she had read about New Orleans. "And the bars have music."

"What kind of music?"

"Mostly jazz."

Keira frowned. "What's jazz?"

"It's music from my parents' time."

"What does it sound like?"

"Oh, I don't know. To me it sounds happy."

"Is it like the music in Mexico?"

"No. But different kinds of music can make you happy."

"What kind of music makes you sad?"

"Country music makes you sad," Lindsey said. "It's about losing the love of your life."

"So was my father the love of your life?"

"Mm, if he was, then you're the child of the love of my life."

Keira smiled, liking that.

After dinner, while Margo cleaned up the kitchen, Lindsey went upstairs with Keira to help her with homework. They returned about an hour later and settled in the living room to watch television, where Margo joined them. There wasn't much for the three of them to watch on the regular channels, so they turned to Netflix and resumed watching a series about a family in England. At nine it was time for Keira to go to bed, so after Margo had confiscated her phone for the night she went upstairs, leaving her mother and her grandmother on the sofa. Together, they tried watching the news but it was so depressing that they switched to a program about elephants in Africa, and by ten they both went upstairs.

Margo still slept on her side of the queen size bed that she had shared with Jack for thirty-five years, and at times she would roll over in the middle of the night expecting to find him there. Before trying to go to sleep she always read for a while because it helped to shut down her mind, and tonight she read another chapter of a novel that Greta had recently lent her. But tonight it didn't shut down her mind, and for a long time she lay awake, wondering what to do about her situation. Though she leaned toward expanding her business she reviewed the alternative of getting a job, and she searched her mind for possibilities. She quickly ruled out working for another doctor having seen from her own experience how receptionist jobs were being eliminated. Just last week she had gone to have blood drawn at a lab in Yonkers for the upcoming appointment with her family doctor, and there wasn't a human being in the reception area, only a machine on a stand where you checked in by entering a code and then one after another placing your driver's license and your health insurance card in a receptacle where the machine could read them. The system worked, but it took her more than twenty minutes to check in as opposed to less than one minute with a live receptionist. Obviously, the owner of the lab had installed the system to reduce costs but at the expense of customers.

Real estate firms still had live agents, but from what she had observed they no longer had secretaries. The agents did their own communications using computers and smartphones. Executives at large corporations probably still had secretaries, but she didn't have a set of current skills for that kind of job, and anyway she was too old to meet the expectations of the men or women at that level. The last time she had called an executive on the phone, the son of a lifelong friend, to tell him that his mother had been taken to the hospital the girl who answered had an English accent.

Reluctantly, she considered a job in retail, where she had worked from time to time between other jobs. Since the stores in Hastings wouldn't have openings it would have to be at a larger store in a strip mall on Central Avenue or a shopping mall in White Plains, which almost always had openings because of their high turnover. Of course they were unlikely to have a position where she could work from eight to three, and even if they did, she couldn't imagine at her age being on her feet all day attending customers. It made her back ache just thinking about it. And that kind of job would pay even less than Lindsey's job.

Remembering the woman at Tierney's who worked for a call center, she considered doing that. The good part would be the flexible hours, which would enable her to be there when Keira got home from school. In fact, if she worked at home it would make a lot of things easier. Still, if the pay was as low as the woman implied, it might not be enough to help pay her property taxes. She needed to find out exactly how much such a job would pay.

The last job she considered before she finally went to sleep was driving an Uber. At least that made her laugh.

The next morning she got up at six o'clock as usual. Before going downstairs she went into the spare bedroom that she used as an office and sat down at her computer. As usual she turned it on with the intention of checking her email, but for some reason the computer wouldn't do anything. She scrolled and clicked but she couldn't make it work, and then she realized that Microsoft was updating her software. She couldn't understand why they always had to update it. Were they always finding flaws? And if so, why had they released a flawed product? Why hadn't they checked it and fixed it before selling it? Like so many other large companies, including those who made cars and airplanes, they rushed their products to the market before they were ready so they could make money sooner, always at the expense of customers. If she served food in her restaurant before it was properly cooked she would go out of business, but those companies had so much money they could survive almost anything.

Not having time to wait for the update to be completed, she went downstairs and into the kitchen, where she started making coffee. She got a bag of muffins out of the breadbox and put three of them on a plate, and she got a half melon out of the refrigerator, removed its rind, and cut it into bite-sized pieces, which she put into a bowl. And then she got her drug for blood pressure out of the cabinet. It was a diuretic, so she took it in the morning because even without it she had to get up twice during the night to pee. It had been prescribed by Dr. Reilly, who had been her family doctor for a long time but had retired three years ago at the age of sixty-eight. She had tried to talk him out of retiring, but after he described to her the obstacles to being a family practitioner she understood why he was retiring, and she accepted his successor, Dr. Martínez, a woman in her forties whose family had immigrated from Colombia. Dr. Martínez was especially good with Keira, and when she treated the self-inflicted wound in Keira's nose she had talked with her and listened to her and comforted her.

Since she had a slight headache, probably from stress, she reached for the bottle of ibuprofen. It had been a new bottle the last time she used it, and she had had trouble opening it. On the pretext of making bottles of medicine child-proof, the drug companies made them senior-proof with tops you couldn't unlock by pushing them down or squeezing them and sealers you couldn't pry off with a fingernail, so that only a child could open them. Keira, who had been opening senior-proof bottles since she was five, had opened this bottle when it was new, and Margo had sensibly not closed it tight. After flipping off the top she shook out two capsules and swallowed them with water.

When the coffee was ready she poured herself a mug and sat down at the counter and waited. Lindsey was the next one up because she had to leave shortly after seven to get to work by eight, and she dragged herself into the kitchen looking half asleep. Before she did anything else she opened the door of a cabinet and took out the bottles that contained her vitamins as well as her drug for depression. Standing in her bathrobe and flip-flops, she swallowed the pills with a glass of water, and after pouring herself a mug of coffee she collapsed onto her usual chair and stared at the muffins as if she didn't quite know what they were.

"Would you like your muffin toasted?" Margo asked her.

"Yeah. What kind is it?"

"It's blueberry."

"Did you use organic blueberries?"

"Of course I did. And organic flour, organic sugar, organic baking powder, organic baking soda, organic oil, and organic salt." She immediately regretted listing all the organic ingredients that way, but for some reason she was annoyed by her daughter's question.

Lindsey didn't seem to take offense, she only stared at the muffins.

Margo took a muffin from the plate, removed its baking cup, and placed it on the rack in the toaster oven. She put it on bake at a temperature of 350°.

"I didn't get a good night's sleep," Lindsey said.

"Were you worrying about something?"

"No, not really. I was just thinking about how I hate my job."

"Have you thought about looking for another job?"

"I've thought about it, but I don't know what else I could do. I don't have the qualifications for anything else."

"How long have you been at the hospital?"

"Almost twelve years."

"So maybe you could get another job there, at a higher level."

"I couldn't without a master's degree."

Margo paused. "Well, you can still get a master's degree. You completed a year, didn't you?"

"Yeah. But what I learned in those courses is out of date. I'd have to start over."

"You can still do it."

Lindsey shook her head, saying: "No, I can't."

"Then maybe you could apply your experience somewhere else. I mean, working with disturbed children."

"Maybe. What I hate about this job isn't the children, it's the hospital."

"Why do you hate the hospital?"

"Because for them it's all about money. They really don't care about the children, they only care about the money."

"Who pays them?"

"The parents of the children. They're stinking rich, or they couldn't afford that hospital."

"Then you might be happier working for a nonprofit hospital."

"Yeah, I might."

At that moment Keira appeared in the doorway, also looking half asleep, but she managed to say: "Good morning."

"Good morning, honey," Margo said. "Would you like a muffin?"

"Oh, yeah. I love your muffins."

"And how about some hot chocolate?"

Lindsey shook her head, saying: "She shouldn't drink hot chocolate. The caffeine is bad for her."

"There's not much caffeine in hot chocolate."

"There's more than you think. They don't tell you."

"You're drinking coffee," Keira said to her mother, "and that has caffeine in it."

"I need caffeine to wake up."

"Well, maybe I need caffeine to wake up."

Margo could have pointed out that caffeine might help Keira concentrate, but she didn't, she only said: "It won't hurt her."

Lindsey let it pass, but after a long, tense silence she reminded her daughter: "Be sure to take your med."

While Keira took her bottle of pills out of the cabinet Margo started making hot chocolate, using powder, which she mixed thoroughly in a mug with sugar and water. Then she filled the teapot with enough water and set it on the stove over a high flame.

After obediently taking her pill with a swig of water Keira approached the counter and reached for a muffin.

"I could toast that for you," Margo offered.

"Thanks, I'll do it."

By the time Keira took her muffin out of the toaster oven the teapot was beginning to whistle, and Margo finished making the hot chocolate.

"I gotta get dressed," Lindsey said, getting up from the counter.

"I gotta eat my muffin," Keira told her.

"Are your clothes ready for school?"

"Yeah. Don't worry."

Lindsey got up and kissed her daughter on the head before leaving the kitchen. According to the clock on the counter it was quarter to seven, which gave her time to dress for work because she wore scrubs.

Keira, who had plenty of time before she had to leave for school, lingered in the kitchen, eating the muffin and sipping the hot chocolate.

Margo was enjoying a moment of peace.

"Would caffeine help me concentrate?" Keira asked her.

"I don't know. It might."

"Well, then maybe I should drink coffee."

"You're too young to drink coffee," Margo said, repeating what her mother had told her and what she had told her children.

"Why am I too young to drink it?"

"I don't know." It was a good question, one that Margo hadn't asked when she was Keira's age. "I guess because it has caffeine, and caffeine is a drug, and drugs can be bad for you."

"But isn't my med a drug?"

"Yeah, but it was prescribed by a doctor."

Keira paused. "The med I took for depression was prescribed by a doctor, and that wasn't good for me. So how do you know the med I'm taking for ADHD is good for me?"

"We don't really know, but we believe it's good for you."

"Based on what?"

"Based on studies of people who have taken it."

"Do those studies prove it's good for me?"

"They don't prove it, but they indicate that it's good for you."

"For me personally?"

"No, for people like you."

"But no one's exactly like me."

"No one is," Margo said, putting an arm around the girl and hugging her. "You're unique, you're a gift from God."

Keira leaned against her, saying: "I love you, Gram."

"I love you too, honey. And don't forget it."

They were still in the kitchen when Lindsey left for work, and then while Keira got dressed for school Margo cleaned up the kitchen, wondering if she could get a job with a call center.

She left the house with Keira at twenty to eight and walked with her to Five Corners, taking a slightly longer route to the café so she could extend her time with Keira, and then they headed in different directions, with Keira walking up Farragut Parkway and Margo walking down Main Street, resolved to expand her business somehow because at her age she didn't see much possibility of getting a job.

As she walked down Main Street she avoided the side where they were redoing the sidewalks. It was a mess, with nowhere to walk except in the street. The contractor had laid out planks so people could get into the stores, but older people didn't feel safe walking a plank, so they didn't risk it. Margo felt bad for the owners of those businesses, and she worried about how it would affect her café when they started working on Warburton. She didn't understand why they were redoing the sidewalks which she thought had been fine, or why they were ripping out the trees which after thirty years were finally providing shade and comfort. They were making the village bare and desolate for what purpose? As far as she could see, the only purpose was to spend money on this project.

THREE

BY THE TIME SHE arrived at work she had decided to call her oldest daughter, Shannon, and talk with her. Shannon was the most stable of her children, the most sensible, and she might offer some good advice. Since they couldn't meet for lunch then maybe they could meet for dinner at Tierney's where she occasionally went on Friday to meet friends.

Chavo had opened the café, as he often did, and he was already in the kitchen making soup for lunch. Today in addition to the popular chicken noodle he was making an Italian soup with white beans, red cabbage, and sausage, which wasn't ready to be tasted but smelled good. It made her wish they didn't already have two Italian restaurants in the village because she might have extended her hours of operation with Chavo as her partner offering Italian food.

The day began with the usual takeout customers followed by the people who came for breakfast, and it was a while before Margo had an opportunity to call Shannon, who answered after only two rings. She must have seen from the caller ID that it was her mother.

Instead of wasting her daughter's precious time with chitchat, Margo got right to the point and asked Shannon if she was free for dinner on Friday.

"Yeah, I'm free," Shannon said as if she had detected a problem. "Is everything all right?"

"Oh, yeah. But I want to get your advice on something."

"Okay. Where do you want to meet?"

"Let's meet at Tierney's. Would six work for you?"

"Yeah, six would be fine."

"So I'll see you then."

As she ended the call she was thankful that she would be able to talk with Shannon about her situation. Shannon had a degree in business from St. Catherine College, and she had a good job as the manager of a senior complex that included facilities for independent living, assisted living, and a nursing home. It was originally sponsored by the sisters who founded St. Catherine, and it was now owned by a nonprofit corporation that continued the mission of the sisters, two of whom were still on its board. After graduating from college Shannon got a job in the city at a major bank, and she did well, rising to the level of vice president within three years. But she wasn't satisfied with being a banker, so she changed careers and took a job in finance at the nursing home which over the years expanded into the complex that she managed now. She was paid a good salary but nowhere near the level she would have been paid if she had continued working in the private sector, and her husband was paid a minimal salary as a social worker for the city, but together they had enough income to afford their house in Hartsdale and send their two children to a Catholic elementary school, though they didn't have the kind of money that people from the city were bringing to Hastings.

Margo was standing at the counter when a young woman who was sitting at a table on the far side of the room got up and approached her, requesting the password for the internet. Margo assumed that this woman, whom she didn't recognize, was a new customer because the regular customers all knew the password. Providing internet service especially attracted younger people, though people her age also appreciated it, using it mostly for sending and receiving emails. Shortly after she started the café a young man who attended St. Catherine had suggested that she provide the service, and he had helped her set it up. Right now about half of her customers were using the internet, most on phones but a few on laptops.

After giving the password to the woman she remembered that she was going to check with Robert about the legality of the rent increase. She had known Robert since elementary school, where he had been a year ahead of her. His father worked at the

Anaconda plant, so he knew her father. Robert got his law degree from Pace University and started a practice in Hastings serving families and local businesses. His office was in a building down on Spring Street, and unlike so many other people his age he hadn't retired, though he was at his office only on Tuesdays, Wednesdays, and Thursdays, giving him an extended weekend to spend in Stonington, Connecticut, where he kept his sailboat. When she decided to start her business Robert helped her create a limited liability company with her as sole owner, and when she decided to hire Chavo he confirmed that it was legal, he explained the legal and tax requirements of having an employee, and he coordinated with Greta to set up the payroll deductions for Social Security, Medicare, and unemployment insurance. Since it was Friday he wouldn't be at his office today, but she called him anyway and left a message.

The morning went as usual, and when Greta came in for lunch she had an expression on her face that suggested she had an idea which she would reveal in due time. They exchanged greetings, and then Greta went to her usual table in the corner and ordered the soup of the day along with a chicken parmesan wedge.

When Margo was finally able to sit down with her, Greta said: "I figured it out. I'd like to have a Portuguese restaurant like the one we had years ago."

Remembering the meals she had there with her family, Margo said: "Yeah. I miss that place."

"My husband and my kids loved it."

"We have a seafood restaurant, but it's not the same."

"It has oysters and clams and mussels and lobster rolls, but it doesn't have a lot of fish. At the Portuguese restaurant they had all kinds of fish, even whole fish."

"Jack loved the whole fish. There weren't many places where they had whole fish."

"Except Chinese, but that was carp, which Dom didn't like."

"They also had a steak that Jack liked."

"Steak on a stone," Greta recalled.

"And roadside chicken."

"Grilled with garlic."

"Mm, yeah. At a good price."

"And that's another thing. We still have people in this village who aren't rich, so you could offer them good food at a good price."

For a while Margo thought about it, and then she said: "I like the idea. But where would I find a partner for a Portuguese restaurant?"

"In Portugal," Greta joked. "But there must be someone in this area who knows how to run a Portuguese restaurant."

"There's a Portuguese restaurant in Yonkers. Or there was before covid."

"I think it's still there. And there's one in Ossining."

"There was an excellent one in Tarrytown. We used to go there on special occasions."

"Yeah, Dom really liked that place. He always ordered the same thing—shrimp bisque and baked cod."

"Jack usually had the mariscada."

"And Dom always had their molotov dessert."

"Meringue with burnt sugar."

"And they gave you a glass of port after dinner, on the house."

"Yeah, Jack liked that."

"So did Dom."

They were silent for a while, remembering the good times they had at the restaurant with their husbands.

"So maybe," Greta said, "you should contact the owners of the Portuguese restaurants in Yonkers and Ossining and see if they might be interested."

"But they already have businesses. Why would they want to get involved in a new business?"

"They might see it as a good opportunity."

"Or they might see it as competition."

Greta sighed. "Then maybe you could advertise for a partner."

"How? We don't have a newspaper anymore." The paper that had served the River Villages for many years had recently closed. It had been an asset for the community with local stories and letters to the editor and obituaries and school sports. Like so many other local newspapers it had been killed by the internet.

"You could use the internet."

"The internet? I couldn't even use my computer this morning. The nerds were updating my software."

"Yeah, that's a pain. They say it's to improve security."

"There's no security. Every day I get a hacker. Last week someone tried to impersonate my nephew."

"A woman in my building lost her savings to a hacker. He impersonated her grandson, who's in the military stationed in Africa."

"We have troops in Africa?"

"We have them everywhere. Anyway, the hacker told her he'd been kidnapped and he needed money to pay ransom."

"Couldn't she check that story?"

"Yeah, but she would've had to contact the military, and she was told that if she did, they'd kill her grandson. So she wired the money."

"How much money?"

"Thirty thousand dollars."

"Oh, my God. Where did she send it?"

"To an online account."

"And the bank didn't stop her?"

"The bank had her authorization to send the money, which is all they needed. And of course they got a fee for the transfer."

"The poor woman."

"They prey on seniors," Greta said, somehow implying that they weren't the only ones who preyed on seniors.

After another moment of silence Margo said: "Well, I guess I could use our group on Facebook."

"Which group?"

"The one with the zip code of our village." It was where people who needed a carpenter, a plumber, an electrician, a driver, or other service could ask for recommendations.

"Oh, yeah. You could try that. It doesn't cost anything."

"I'm not sure how to post in the group, but my granddaughter could show me how to do it."

"That's what grandchildren are for—to show us how to use the internet."

A customer was signaling her, so she got up. The woman, who lived in an apartment across the street, wanted to order the chicken Milanese to take home for dinner. Margo went into the kitchen to give Chavo the order, and she found him on his phone.

"Is everything all right?" she asked after he ended the call because he almost never used his phone at work.

"Yeah. That was Lupe. She asked me to bring home food for dinner." Lupe, his wife, had taken the semester off from college to be with her baby, and she usually cooked dinner for herself. But maybe today for some reason she just didn't feel like it.

Margo gave him the order for her customer and returned to the front, where she greeted a regular customer, a young man who always brought his laptop and did a lot of typing on it. She took his order for a coffee and a ham sandwich and watched him sit down and open his laptop and start typing. According to Greta he was writing a novel.

After closing at three she added up the chits and found that it had been another good day, though still not enough to pay double the rent. She locked up and walked down Warburton, and after crossing Spring Street she stopped at the large building at the corner. Years ago it was the Hastings House, a popular local bar and restaurant, where she went every Sunday with her family after Mass to have brunch. At the time her father still had his job as a section manager at the Anaconda plant, so they could afford to have brunch here and also have dinner now and then at the Italian restaurant on Main Street. Back then, as far as she could remember, there were only two restaurants in the village because people didn't eat out so often, but there were twelve bars serving the two thousand men who worked at the Anaconda plant in three shifts, which ended at four in the afternoon, at midnight, and at eight in the morning, so the men who didn't go home directly after work could go to a bar no matter which shift they were on. Before his promotion to section manager Margo's father had alternating shifts, the most disruptive one of which was from midnight to eight because he had to get his sleep during the day and the children had to avoid making a sound that might disturb him. Since Margo was the oldest her mother always relied on her to help control her three siblings.

Peering through the window at the raw cement floor where the bar and restaurant used to be, she remembered how her father worked here as a bartender after he lost his job at the Anaconda plant, a few years before it finally closed. As a teenager she had peered through this window and seen him standing behind the bar and regaling customers with stories in his Irish brogue, which he retained after living in America for so many years. He was born in Northern Ireland, one of eleven children in a Catholic family living on a farm, and he came here at the age of eighteen seeking a better life. It didn't take him long to get a menial job at the plant, and he commuted by train from Yonkers where he lived in a two-family house near McLean Avenue with his uncle and aunt. Three years after his arrival he was drafted into the army, and he served with the tank corps in North Africa. After the war he returned to Yonkers, and he resumed working at the plant, where five years later he met a young woman who worked there in the office. She also lived in Yonkers, on Willow Steet near Our Lady of Mt. Carmel, and she also commuted by train, but they didn't meet on the train because her job was nine to five, so they didn't come and go at the same time. He met her because he had to go to the office and straighten out a problem with his record. They dated for three years and then they got married and lived with his uncle and aunt until their second child was on the way. At that point he was earning enough as a section manager to afford a house, and after looking around for a while they found the house in Hastings, which among its many advantages reduced his commuting time. So they moved to Hastings when Margo was two.

Now, as she peered through the window, she was saddened by what had happened to this building. Almost fifteen years ago an investor purchased it with the bright idea of turning it into a catering hall, but the village didn't approve the project because of its failure to provide the required parking. The building sat idle for a while until another investor purchased it with another bright idea, and he replaced the old windows and rebuilt the main floor before he evidently ran out of money. So for all those years the building, which had once been a hub of the village, had been empty and devoid of life.

She turned away and continued north on Warburton. She crossed Broadway after waiting for the light and walked to her street where, turning into it, she saw the gray van with ladders on top and the huge black pickup truck on her side of the street. They were there every day except Sunday, working on the house across the street that a couple had bought almost two years ago for two million dollars, according to a neighbor who knew the agent who had sold it to them. The husband worked on Wall Street doing something with securities and obviously making a ton of money, which his wife was spending on the house. Margo had never met the woman, but she had seen her a few times. The last time was a few weeks ago when she had arrived in her Mercedes, as usual wearing fashionable clothes. She had brought a woman who followed her into the house carrying a portfolio. From what she had observed, Margo guessed that the wife fancied herself as a designer, and that the house was her latest project. According to the neighbor who had told her how much they paid for the house, the couple lived in Manhattan on the Upper East Side, and they had bought the house as an investment. So at some point in the future they would sell the house, hoping to make a profit on it but also hoping to have it featured in a magazine. What they were doing wouldn't have bothered Margo except that their overpayment for the house had enabled the town to increase the assessment of her house, which increased her taxes, and every day except Sunday their work crew occupied scarce parking places on the street.

When she got the mail on her way into the house she saw that among the catalogs and other junk there was a letter from the Town of Greenburgh, in which the village was situated. As far as she could see, the only purpose of the town was to collect taxes and pay its officials exorbitant salaries because they didn't provide any services to the village. At least the county, to which she paid higher taxes, provided a useful bus service, repaired roads, and operated a community college so she didn't mind paying taxes to them, up to a point.

She let herself into the house and went into the kitchen where she opened the letter from the Town of Greenburgh, which informed her that they were going to increase the assessment of her house by thirty percent.

"What?" she cried aloud. "You can't do that."

But she knew they could, and even though they said she could appeal the increase she had gone through that process a few years ago and found that after hours of preparing her case it got her nowhere. They claimed that their figure was the market value of her house, and that it had been determined objectively by a professional firm. They also claimed that an increase in assessment didn't necessarily mean an increase in taxes because if her increase was the same as the average increase on houses in her area, it wouldn't affect her taxes, which were affected only by the budgets of the county, the town, the village, and the school district. But her taxes kept increasing along with the assessments, so if Jack was still around he would have said their claim was a crock of shit.

Stunned by this second blow, she sat down at the counter. They were not only doubling the rent on her business, they were also increasing the taxes on her house. They were trying to drive her out of her home. And why? Did they believe that her house could be used for a better purpose if it was occupied by a young family? Did they want her to go away and die? Did they care about their own mothers and grandmothers? Did they care about anything but money?

"God damn you!" she said aloud, referring to the people who had paid two million dollars for the house across the street. It was people like them who provided the unreal figures that assessors claimed were market value. At least for a moment she hated those people, and then, repenting, she said: "God forgive me."

She was still sitting at the counter, feeling depressed, when Keira popped into the kitchen, saying: "Hi, Gram."

"Hi, honey," she said, trying to sound happy.

"Are you all right?" Keira asked, scanning her face.

"Yeah, I'm all right."

"You don't look happy."

Seeing an opportunity for education, she said: "Well, I'm not happy about what I just learned from the town."

"What did you just learn from the town?" Keira asked, approaching her.

"They're going to raise the taxes on our house."

"What are taxes?"

"Taxes are money I pay to the village, the town, the county, and the school district for services they provide us."

"I thought the school was free."

"They don't charge tuition, but they need money to pay the teachers and other expenses, so they collect taxes from homeowners."

"Would you have to pay those taxes if I wasn't here going to the school?"

"Oh, yeah. You have to pay them if you own a house in the school district, even if you never have a child going to school."

"That doesn't sound fair," Keira said, sitting at the counter. Since she hadn't paused to get a cookie she must have been really interested in the conversation.

"I think it's fair because it spreads the cost of the school among all the homeowners in the district."

"So all the homeowners have to pay something?"

"That's right. We all have to pay something."

"But how do they decide how much you have to pay?"

Attempting to find a simple way to explain it, she said: "The amount you pay is based on the market value of your house."

"What's market value?"

"It's what a house would sell for."

"Well, what would this house sell for?"

"I have no idea, but it wouldn't be enough for us to live on."

"Then you don't plan to sell it?"

"No. I plan to stay here as long as I can."

"That's good," Keira told her, "because I don't want to live anywhere else."

"I don't either."

Keira finally got a cookie, and munching it she sat down again at the counter and asked: "How much did you pay for this house?"

"I didn't pay anything. My parents bought it two years after I was born."

"And you've lived here ever since?"

"I lived in Yonkers for a while after I was married, but I moved back here a few months before your mother was born."

"So that was more than thirty years ago."

"Yeah." At the time they were living in Jack's one-bedroom apartment on Lake Avenue in Yonkers, and though Jack had at first resisted the idea of living with her parents he came around and eventually adapted to the situation.

"So you didn't have to pay anything for this house."

"No, but I still have to pay the expenses of maintaining it."

"What kind of expenses?"

"Gas, electric, insurance, repairs, and taxes."

"What's the biggest expense?"

"Taxes. They're more than all the other expenses put together."

"That sucks," Keira said with empathy.

Deciding that for now her granddaughter had gotten enough education on real life, she suggested that they play checkers, and they were in their third game when Lindsey got home, as usual looking wiped out.

Margo didn't have to ask how her day was, and silently she prayed that Lindsey would start looking for a job.

On Friday, after leaving a prepared dinner for Lindsey and Keira, she left the house and walked to Tierney's, which was on

Warburton just south of the post office. Tierney's was the only remaining bar from the era when the village had twelve bars, and it was more than a bar now after being remodeled by the present owner. Instead of the booths that had lined the wall opposite the bar there were high tops, and in the back there were tables. And instead of being limited to burgers, wings, and fish and chips, the menu offered some additional items, including kale and Brussel sprouts, though Margo knew from conversations with the regulars that those items weren't very popular but were on the menu to attract people who had moved to Hastings from the city. But few of them came to Tierney's, they went to places like Gotham on the corner of Spring Street where they could spend twice as much for upscale fare, and where they could pretend they were hanging out on the Upper East Side.

When she turned eighteen, the legal age for drinking at that time, she had her first legal drink at the Hastings House where her father worked as a bartender after losing his job at Anaconda. Of course it wasn't her first drink because for the past two years she and Greta had been furtively going to a dive south of the bridge with their fake IDs and drinking Screwdrivers, but her father hadn't known about that, so she innocently sought his advice on what to order, and he suggested Guinness, which he always had, and she liked it. From then on Margo and her father would meet on Friday after work for a drink at Tierney's, where they would drink Guinness together and talk.

Tonight she was greeted at Tierney's by a young woman with tattoos on her arms who knew her from times she had come here before. She would arrive early and take a seat at the end of the bar, which gave her a complete view of the place, including all the tables in back, and she would order Guinness, which she sipped until she was joined by a friend. They would talk for a while, and then they would order food. She always had something she didn't have at her café, such as cod, or salmon, or mussels. Though she was allowed to have meat on Friday, except during Lent, she still avoided it out of habit. And now it was Lent.

Since she was meeting Shannon she asked the hostess for a table in back, where it was less noisy, and a few minutes after she sat at a table Yesenia, a young Latina who worked there as a second job, brought water and a menu and asked her if she would like something to drink. And as usual she ordered Guinness.

She was sipping her drink when Shannon appeared, wearing a navy blue suit and looking like an executive. Shannon leaned over and kissed her, saying: "I'm sorry I'm late."

"You're not late. It's only four minutes after six."

"Well, I like to be exactly on time," Shannon said, sitting down opposite her.

"Your hair looks great," Margo told her. It was naturally blond but since Shannon was thirty-nine now it benefited from a mild highlighting.

"Thank you. And so does yours."

For years she had resisted letting her hair turn gray, but about two years ago she had stopped coloring it, and now she only had to use a special shampoo every few weeks to stop the white from turning yellow.

"So how are your kids?" Margo asked, not having seen them since Christmas when Shannon hosted the family dinner. They were thirteen and eleven.

"They're fine. Patty's involved in a program to deliver food to the poor, and Sean's involved in a science project."

"That's wonderful. I assume they're doing well in school."

"Oh, yeah. They must have inherited their brains from Conor."

"You did well in school."

"I did okay, but not as well as Lindsey."

"She did do well in school," Margo said, "but she's not doing so well now."

"She still has her job, doesn't she?"

"Yeah, but she hates working for that hospital."

"She should get another job."

"I think she should. And maybe you can encourage her."

"Would you like something to drink?" Yesenia asked Shannon.

"Yeah. I'll have a white wine, please."

"Would you like Chardonnay or Sauvignon blanc?"

"Chardonnay, please." Then after a pause Shannon asked: "Why does she hate working for that hospital?"

"She says they only care about money."

"I understand. I feel blessed that we're still committed to the mission of the sisters."

"I told her she might be happier at a nonprofit hospital."

"She might, but she'd have to deal with the politics."

"But don't you have to deal with the politics?"

"Yeah. But I'm used to it."

"Well, I have to deal with something," Margo said, broaching the subject.

Shannon looked worried. "I hope you don't have a health problem."

"No, it's not my health, thank God. It's my business. The new owner of my building is going to double my rent."

"What? Is that legal?"

"I'm afraid it is. I have an option to renew my lease for another five years, but at the market rent."

"And the market rent is double what you're paying now?"

"That's what they claim," Margo said. "It seems like the market value of everything is increasing a lot. According to the Town of Greenburgh, the market value of my house has increased by thirty percent."

"So you got their letter?"

"I got it two days ago."

"We got our letter yesterday," Shannon said, "and they increased our assessment. But they say that if the assessments of all the houses in the town are increased by the same percentage, it doesn't increase our taxes."

"If it doesn't increase our taxes, then why are they doing it?"

"They say they're doing it to make things fair."

"But property taxes are never fair. They're not based on your income, they're based on what people with a lot of money pay for houses in your neighborhood."

"Oh, I agree. So we have to change the system. But in the meantime how are you going to deal with your rent increase?"

"That's what I wanted to talk about, but let's order."

When they had made their decisions Margo signaled Yesenia, and they placed their orders: salmon for Margo and cod for Shannon. And then they resumed their conversation.

"As you know," Margo said, "the income from my business helps me pay my property taxes. But if my new landlord doubles my rent, then I won't make enough money from my business, and I might even lose money."

"You'll lose money," Shannon said. She knew because she helped Margo prepare her taxes with the bookkeeping information that Greta produced.

"That's what I thought. So I gotta find another source of income to help pay my taxes."

"Have you thought about selling the house?"

"Yeah, but I've ruled that out because I wouldn't get enough from the sale to buy or rent an apartment with three bedrooms in this area."

"Why wouldn't you?"

"Because I'd have to share the proceeds with my siblings."

"Mm. Well, you have children who could help you."

"That's not the solution. Lindsey's contributing as much as she can, and Tricia's always living on the edge, so that leaves you, and in a few years your kids will be in Catholic high schools, which will cost a lot of money."

"They could go to the public high school."

"Oh, no. You're not going to sacrifice their future for me."

"Okay. So you've ruled out selling the house. Now, what are your other alternatives?"

"Well, I could close the business and get a job."

"Yeah, you could. What kind of job?"

"A job that requires people skills."

"Like working in an office. But you also have experience in managing a restaurant."

"I never thought of that," Margo said, intrigued. "I like that better than working in an office."

"So apply for a job managing a restaurant."

"How would I do that?" She hadn't applied for a job since her first one out of business school. After that she had gotten her jobs through referrals.

"Write a resume and post it online."

"Where online?"

"I could give you some websites." Shannon reached into her pocketbook and took out her phone. She found what she was looking for. "I'll email them to you. Okay?"

"Okay." But she was already wondering if there were jobs with the hours she needed.

Their food arrived, and they started eating.

"The other alternative," Margo said after swallowing a bite of perfectly cooked salmon, "is to extend the hours of my business and serve dinner as well as breakfast and lunch."

"What kind of food would you serve for dinner?"

"Greta suggested Portuguese."

"Like the Portuguese restaurant we used to have here?"

"Yeah. Remember?"

Shannon nodded. "We went there often. We always started with fried calamari. And Dad always had a whole fish."

"We had a lot of good times at that restaurant."

"Yeah, we did."

She was silent for a while, remembering the good times they had there as a family, and then she said: "So maybe I could serve Portuguese food. But I'd have to find a partner."

"Yeah. Someone who knows Portuguese food."

"And someone who could take over in the afternoon."

Shannon nodded. "How's Keira doing?"

"She's doing better. And there's certainly nothing wrong with her brain. She beats me more than half the time at checkers."

"You can't leave her alone at home?"

"No, I can't. And anyway I couldn't work from eight in the morning until ten at night."

"So you could look for a partner at those websites I sent you. I use them all the time to hire people."

She felt better not only about getting a job but also about finding a partner. And she reached across the table and took her daughter's hand, saying: "Thanks. I knew you could help me."

As she was walking home her phone rang, and it was Robert calling from the marina where he kept his boat. He knew the terms of her lease, and he told her sadly that she would have to pay whatever her landlord determined was the market rent. She could fight it, but in his experience the rulings in such cases were almost always in favor of the landlord.

She appreciated his calling her on a day off, and she thanked him and wished him good weather for sailing.

Before breakfast the next morning she drafted a resume on her computer and emailed it to Shannon for review. She also located the two websites that Shannon had given her, and she figured out how to post on them to find a job as well as to find a partner. By the end of the day she received her edited resume from Shannon, and that evening after dinner she posted it to find a job. She also posted a want ad for someone to manage a Portuguese restaurant, with its location, its hours, and its scope.

The next day, Sunday, the café was closed. It was Chavo's day off, and in any case she wouldn't have done much business on Sunday because some people still went to church and most of the other restaurants in the village offered brunch. She went to Mass on Sunday, as she had done for as far back as she could remember, going with her father, her mother, and her siblings. The only problem now was Lindsey, who resisted going and at times refused, saying it didn't do anything for her. At times Margo went without her, but she always took Keira, who did get something out of it. In fact, Margo thought it helped the girl a lot more than her medication. Today Lindsey refused to go, and Keira, who always wanted the family to go to Mass together, tried but couldn't change her mother's mind.

When Keira had left them in Lindsey's bedroom Margo said: "You know, you're not helping your daughter."

"How am I not helping her?"

"You're not setting a good example."

"You want me to be a hypocrite to set a good example?"

"I don't want you to be a hypocrite, I only want you to set a good example."

"Well, if I don't believe in it, how can I set a good example? You want me to pretend I believe in it?"

"No. But since when don't you believe in it?"

"Since a long time ago," Lindsey said with lowered eyes.

"You mean since your divorce?"

"No, I mean before."

"But you always went to Mass before, so were you pretending to believe in it?"

Lindsey sighed. "I wasn't pretending. But at some point it no longer did anything for me."

"Well, it's not just for you."

"I know it's not. It's also for Keira."

"So pull yourself together," Margo told her, "and come with us. It won't hurt you."

Lindsey finally joined them, and they sat in the pew where they had sat when their family was still intact. It was the third pew from the front, on the left, a location established by her father who didn't want his family to be like the people who sat in back on the right side out of the pastor's line of vision when he delivered the homily, some of whom arrived just in time for the Gospel. He wanted them to sit where the pastor could see them and confirm their presence. Margo believed that his need to be acknowledged as present at Mass had something to do with his having belonged to the Catholic minority in Northern Ireland.

At the time when she went to Mass as a child with her family the church was packed, but over the years there were fewer and fewer people there, and now the pews were only about half filled, with a lot of white-haired women like her. As she sang the gathering hymn she glanced around and noticed people she knew, including Greta, who were mostly descendants of the Irish, Italian, and Polish immigrants who had labored in the factories on the riverfront. Back then the church had a nearby elementary school, and Margo and her siblings as well as her children went to that school, but it closed the year after Tricia graduated, so it wasn't there for Keira, and now it was an empty building that the parish still had to maintain.

About ten years ago the parish was merged with a parish in Ardsley, presumably because of the shortage of priests. In fact, for a while the parish imported priests from Ghana, and Margo remembered them fondly. But they were gone, and now the merged parish had a pastor who had been there for the past two years, and he had done a lot to restore the building after so many years of deferred maintenance. The pews had been refinished, the kneelers and the carpets had been replaced, and the latest improvement was the set of elegant overhead lights, which had been rescued from a demolished church in the city. Encouraged by the pastor, people who stopped going to Mass during covid were gradually returning, though the number of active parishioners was still below its precovid level. And the people who were moving here from the city, replacing the people who had grown up here, evidently didn't practice a religion, which made her wonder what would happen to the church after her generation was gone.

As she followed the prayers and the readings Margo was glad that Lindsey had joined them, and she hoped that attending Mass would do something for her. As usual she was mystified by a difference between her three daughters. Shannon attended Mass regularly, Tricia claimed to be an atheist, while Lindsey was in the middle, as she was in other respects, and she could veer one way or the other.

FOUR

WITHIN A WEEK after posting on the websites Margo had a few possibilities for a job as well as for a partner. The possible jobs were all inconveniently far from Hastings, except for the job as assistant manager of a fast-food restaurant in Yonkers. The possible partners were harder to evaluate, but one of them caught her attention—a guy named Donal O'Rourke who was presently managing an Irish pub in Manhattan. And she contacted him to schedule an interview.

The only time that worked for her was at six on a weekday, so she proposed that they meet at that time on Wednesday or Thursday at Tierney's, and since Wednesday also worked for him they agreed to meet then.

On Wednesday after leaving prepared food for Lindsey and Keira she walked to Tierney's, and seeing no one who looked like the photo on Donal's resume she took a seat at the end of the bar and ordered Guinness. She had told him she had white hair so he could spot her.

About ten minutes later she heard behind her a voice with an Irish accent say: "Mrs. Walsh?"

She turned and saw a man in his early thirties with dark wavy hair and beguiling blue eyes. "Hi, are you Donal?"

"I'm Donal. It's a pleasure to meet you." He extended his hand, and when she shook it she felt as if she was being courted.

"Let's go to a table," she suggested, "so we can have some privacy."

"Wherever you want," he said, stepping back to allow her to lead the way.

She took her drink to a table in the far corner where it would be less noisy, and she sat down with her back to the bar. After ordering Guinness he said: "I like this village. It reminds me of where I grew up."

"Where did you grow up?"

"I grew up in a village near Dublin."

"My father came from Ireland."

"Really?" he said. "Where in Ireland?"

"In a rural area near Belfast. He was Catholic," she added.

"I understand. It was hard for us there. It still is."

Yesenia brought his Guinness, which he took a sip of. "Now, that's a good pour. Is the bartender Irish?"

"He's half Irish."

"Well, he knows what he's doing."

She paused for a moment, and then she said: "So you're managing an Irish pub in Manhattan. How long have you been doing that?"

"For more than five years."

"Do you like your job?"

"Oh, yes. I love it."

"Then why do you want to leave it?"

"I have a relationship with a girl who lives in Yonkers, and I plan to move there, so I want a position closer to home."

"Where does your girlfriend live in Yonkers?"

"Near McLean Avenue."

"My father lived in that neighborhood after he came to America."

"I like it there. They have some great Irish pubs."

His answers to her questions were all good, though maybe they were too good. There was something that bothered her, so she continued by asking: "Do you know anything about Portuguese food?"

"I know a lot about it," he said. "I worked in the kitchen of a restaurant in Lisbon for almost two years."

"Why did you go to Lisbon?"

"To get out of Ireland. You know, like James Joyce."

She knew who James Joyce was, though she had never read him. "So you learned how to cook Portuguese food?"

"Yeah, all those fish, including bacalao."

"Do you like Portuguese food?"

"Oh, yes," he said. "There's a Portuguese restaurant near where I live in Manhattan, and I go there often."

"What about your girlfriend? Does she like Portuguese food?"

"She's Portuguese. She introduced me to it."

The more he told her, the more she wondered if he was giving her a line. It was all too good to be true. "Where does she work?"

"She works for a big bank in the city."

"So she commutes from Yonkers?"

"Yes, but when I move there she'll get a job in Yonkers."

"It sounds like you're serious."

"We are," he said. "We're going to get married."

"Congratulations." She hoped that his girlfriend wasn't already pregnant as Lindsey had been when she got married.

"Thank you," he said graciously.

They kept talking, with her asking questions and him giving her good answers. When he had finished his Guinness he looked as if he wanted to have another, but Margo felt they had talked enough. "Well, I just have to check your references. Okay?"

"Okay." He smiled as if he expected to get the job.

Over the next two days she called the references he had given. They all said good things about him, but upon questioning it turned out that none of them knew him from work, they only knew him as a friend.

She finally called the pub listed on his resume, and she talked with a man who claimed to be the manager. He told her that Donal worked there as a bartender, not as a manager, and he had been there less than a year. So if he had lied about that he must have lied about other things. Out of courtesy she called him and thanked him for meeting with her, and she told him she had found someone else. She kept looking but by the beginning of Holy Week she wasn't any closer to finding a job for herself or finding a partner.

The Hastings schools had their spring break during Holy Week, so Margo scheduled Keira to spend three days at the café and two days with Lisa, her best friend, whose mother worked as a teacher's aide at the elementary school, so she was at home because of the break. On the days when Keira was at the café Margo had her set and clear tables, bring food from the kitchen, and replenish cups of coffee. While she wasn't busy Keira sat in a chair next to the counter where she read a book that Margo had found at the library. At times she joined Greta, who welcomed her company and treated her like a granddaughter.

The week passed without any promising leads for a job or a partner, and Margo was acutely conscious of the fact that March was almost over, leaving only two more months for her to find a way to help pay her property taxes and avoid having to sell her house.

She closed the café an hour early on Good Friday so she and Keira could attend the service at St. Matthew at three o'clock. They sat in their usual pew, three rows from the front on the left side, with Keira on the outside so she was in the middle when Lindsey joined them, coming from work with only a few minutes to spare. As usual Keira actively participated, singing in a steady voice the response to the psalm, "Father, into your hands I commend my spirit," and she stood without fidgeting during the long narrative of the Passion from the Gospel of John. She followed her mother in line for the adoration of the cross, and then for communion. And she was solemn when they left the church.

For dinner they had baked cod with rice and zucchini, and the next day while Lindsey and Keira extended their sleep Margo went to the café at the usual time. While keeping an eye on her customers she reviewed the list of items she needed at the supermarket for the family dinner she was hosting the next day. Her mother had always hosted Easter dinner, and Margo continued the tradition, building the menu around leg of lamb, which her mother had taught her to prepare.

After closing the café she went home. She usually walked to the supermarket but today, with a leg of lamb, enough potatoes to feed ten people, plus other items, there was too much to carry, so she took the car with Keira joining her. She hadn't used the car for a while, a Chevy Malibu that she and Jack had bought more than eighteen years ago. Their previous car, with almost two hundred thousand miles, had reached the point where it was no longer reliable, so they went across the river to a dealer in New Jersey whose remaining current-year models were on sale to make room for the new models, and they managed to get a twenty percent discount on this car. According to the local mechanic, who had done the annual inspection a month ago, it would be good for many more years as long as she changed the oil regularly.

The supermarket, which used to be an A&P, was owned by Dominicans who operated several units of a cooperative based in New Jersey. Its customers were people who had lived in Hastings for years and people who lived in Greystone, where a row of high-rise apartment buildings had been developed at the edge of the river. Since there were no stores or restaurants near that location the people who lived there came to Hastings to shop and eat out, and they were essential for the village's commerce. People like her neighbors up the street who had recently moved to the village from the city didn't deign to shop at this supermarket but ordered their groceries online and had them delivered in refrigerated trucks which noisily backed into the street because there wasn't room to turn around.

With the shopping cart Keira followed Margo through the aisles of the supermarket, and she resisted all the temptations for buying sweets. When they got home she carried the bag with the leg of lamb into the house, and she helped Margo put things away. At that point since Margo didn't feel like cooking dinner she invited Lindsey and Keira to have dinner at Tierney's, where they all had fish and chips.

On Easter Sunday they went to the eleven-thirty Mass, and when they got home she changed into work clothes and began the process of making dinner. The first task was peeling and cutting cloves of garlic into slivers that she inserted into the lamb while the oven preheated. After putting the lamb into the oven she enlisted Keira in the task of peeling potatoes and cutting them into pieces for roasting. Then, after washing and cutting up the green beans, she got the shrimp out of the refrigerator and peeled them, deveined them, and dropped them into a pot of salted water that she had brought to a boil and then turned off. Five minutes later she removed the shrimp and plunged them into a bowl of ice water, and when they had cooled she put them back into the refrigerator.

Everything was ready, and she had changed into a dress by the time Shannon arrived with her husband, Conor, and their two children, Patty and Sean, all dressed for church. Then came her brother, Patrick, and his wife, Donna, also dressed for church. And then her youngest daughter, Tricia, who wasn't dressed for church. They hung out in the kitchen, with the adults drinking beer and wine and the children imbibing nonalcoholic spritzers. It wasn't long before the noise level had reached the point where they almost had to shout to be heard.

Keira helped bring the food to the table, and when they were all sitting down Margo said grace, then silently gave thanks for her family and prayed for those who were no longer there.

By the middle of the following week she was almost resigned to selling her house when an Asian man came into her café. He looked about thirty, with a lean body and a handsome face. He ordered a coffee and a croissant, and he sat at a table. Instead of taking out his phone he looked around as if he was interested in what was happening here.

Since the lunch hour was winding down she went over to his table and asked: "Would you like some more coffee?"

"No, thank you," he said politely. "Are you the owner?"

"Yeah," she said, afraid that he was a food inspector who had come to inform her of a violation.

"How long have you had this business here?"

She noticed that he had an English accent. "At the end of next month it'll be five years."

"The sign on the front door says you're open from eight to three. Right?"

"Right. We only do breakfast and lunch."

"Why don't you do dinner?"

"I can only be here until three. And I always made enough money doing breakfast and lunch."

He frowned slightly. "But you must pay a high rent for all this space."

"I do," she said, and trusting him she added: "And after next month I'll have to pay double what I'm paying now."

"Will you be able to pay it?"

"No. I'll have to close my business."

"That would be a shame." He paused, and then asked: "Have you thought of extending your business hours?"

"I have. I've been trying to find a partner to manage a restaurant in the evening."

"And you haven't found one?"

"No, I haven't."

"What kind of food would the restaurant serve?"

"Portuguese food. We had a Portuguese restaurant here for many years, and it did a good business, but the owner retired and went back to Portugal."

"Mm," he said, gazing at her hopefully. "Have you thought about a Chinese restaurant?"

"No. We already have a Chinese restaurant."

"It's only for takeout. And it's not bad, but it's not a place where people can sit down and enjoy a good meal."

After examining his face she asked: "Are you Chinese?"

He nodded. "Yes. But before you ask, I don't have any experience managing a Chinese restaurant. I only have experience working as a waiter in a Chinese restaurant."

"Which restaurant?"

He mentioned an upscale place on Central Avenue.

From the way he looked and talked he didn't seem like a waiter in a Chinese restaurant, so she asked: "Are you working as a waiter while you go to school?"

He laughed and said: "I finished school a while ago. I have a degree in journalism."

"So why are you working as a waiter?"

"Can you keep a secret?"

"Yeah, I can."

"I'm an illegal immigrant seeking asylum."

"An immigrant? From China?"

"From Hong Kong," he said, "which unfortunately was taken over by China."

She knew that Hong Kong had been a British colony, so that explained his English accent. "Why did you leave Hong Kong?"

"It's a long story, but in short I left to avoid going to prison."

"Prison? What for?"

"For defending democracy," he told her.

"Lord have mercy. Do you have family there?"

"Oh, yes. I have a mother, a father, a wife, and two children. They all urged me to leave instead of going to prison."

"I'm sorry," she said with feeling.

He smiled almost brightly, saying: "Don't be sorry. It could be a blessing for you."

"It could? How?"

"I could help you extend your business hours."

"By opening a Chinese restaurant here?"

"Exactly. You said you can only be here until three, so I could run the restaurant from four until ten."

Intrigued, she asked: "Who would do the cooking?"

"I could find a chef, ideally someone who came from Hong Kong. So we speak the same language," he added.

"You don't all speak the same language?"

"In theory we all speak Mandarin," he explained, "but most people speak their regional language, and they don't understand other regional languages, which can be as different as German and French."

"I never knew that."

"Luckily for me, most of the Chinese in this area speak Cantonese, which is what we speak in Hong Kong."

She gazed at him, wondering if he was a blessing or a clever scamster, but instinctively believing he was the former. At that moment she noticed a cord around his neck, which at its end could have had a cross, a picture of his wife, or a lucky charm.

"So what do you say?" he asked her.

"About what?" she said, stalling.

"About being partners?"

"Can you give me references?"

"Well, I can give you the name of the guy who manages the restaurant where I work. And I can give you the name of the editor of the newspaper where I worked in Hong Kong, but it would take a long time for you to hear back from him."

"Because he's in prison?"

"Right. Doing fifteen years."

"So what's your name?"

"Anthony Chen. What's yours?"

"Margo Walsh."

They shook hands.

That night she lay awake thinking about Anthony's idea. It wasn't what she had hoped for, but it was something, and she had less than two months to exercise her option to renew the lease. Within that time it was unlikely that she would find another partner, or that she would find a job, so maybe she had nothing to lose by going into business with Anthony—except that she would be on the hook for a doubled rent, which could ruin her.

Anthony had come out of the blue, and she knew nothing about him other than what he had told her, so it all came down to whether she could trust him. She wished there was a way she could verify his story, but the only way was to call the restaurant where he said he worked, which wouldn't tell her much and might get him into trouble. She would just have to make a leap of faith. But even then she would still have the risk of opening a Chinese restaurant in the village. And how would Anthony, a stranger, know if there was a need for such a restaurant?

She didn't get much sleep that night, and the next day as the lunch hour was winding down she joined Greta, who had finished her soup and saved half of her wedge to take home.

"So what's happening?" Greta asked her.

"Well," Margo said, "a guy came in yesterday, a Chinese guy—"

"A Chinese guy?"

"Yeah, and he said I should have a Chinese restaurant here in the evening."

"Does he know we already have a Chinese restaurant?"

"He said it was only for takeout, but we need a place where people can sit down and enjoy a good meal."

"What does he know about our village?" Greta said skeptically.

"I don't know. But he must know something, or he wouldn't have come here."

"Where did he come from?"

"He said he came from Hong Kong."

"And you believe him?"

"Yeah, I believe him."

Greta frowned. "So how long has he been in this country?"

"He didn't say, but I have a feeling he hasn't been here long. He works as a waiter at a Chinese restaurant on Central Avenue."

"A waiter? Then he could be an illegal immigrant."

"He said he is. He said he came here seeking asylum."

"Asylum from what?"

"From going to prison."

"Wow. That's a tall story."

"But I feel it's true. I mean, he seems like a nice young man."

"Maybe he is, but he could be a con man."

"I know. But I don't think he is."

Greta paused, and then said: "Okay. Assume he's for real, but why does he think we need a Chinese restaurant here?"

"I don't know. But he seems pretty sure that we need one."

"Well, we never had a Chinese restaurant here, except for the takeout. And there must have been a reason."

"Maybe no one had the idea."

"Maybe. But maybe people who had the idea realized that there was competition from the Chinese restaurants in Dobbs Ferry and Ardsley."

"There's competition from the Italian restaurants in those villages," Margo pointed out, "but we have two of them here."

"Okay. But they're doubling your rent," Greta reminded her. "Do you really believe you'd get enough income from a Chinese restaurant to pay that rent?"

"I don't know. I hope I would."

Greta was silent for a while, and then she said: "Well, maybe you could reduce your risk."

"I'd like to, but how?"

"You could renew your lease for one year at double the rent, with an option to renew for four more years."

"You think my new landlord would do that?"

"He might. I mean, he'd get the rent he wants, and if you didn't renew he could find another tenant."

"So I'd only be on the hook for one year."

"It would give you time to see if this restaurant is successful. When restaurants fail," Greta added, based on her experience, "they usually fail in their first year."

"Okay. I'll try it," Margo said. "Do you have any other ideas?"

"Yeah, I do. The restaurant and the café should be separate businesses, and your partner should sublet from you, paying half the rent and utilities."

"And you'd be the bookkeeper for both businesses."

"To keep you both honest," Greta said, smiling.

"So I'll call Anthony and ask him to meet with me. Do I need a lawyer?"

"What for? If he's a con man, it won't do any good to have a legal agreement with him. And if he's an illegal immigrant, he won't want a lawyer involved."

"Okay. Thanks."

That evening after having dinner she got a phone call from Tricia, who didn't call her often. They had talked at Easter, but Tricia hadn't said anything about quitting her job and going on a trip with her Mexican boyfriend. Margo had met the boyfriend, Diego, when Tricia brought him to Tierney's on a Friday evening. He was a suave young man, and with his light skin and slim body he didn't look like the Mexicans who worked for the landscaping services that people now used instead of mowing their own lawns. He looked European, and he spoke English with only the slightest accent. He also dressed well and projected an image of being wealthy. But Margo wasn't impressed by this guy, the latest in a series of boyfriends since Tricia was in high school. At that time she wondered if Tricia was offering sex to attract them, but Lindsey assured her that Tricia was only teasing them and leading them on.

"Hi, Mom," Tricia said in her young voice. "How're things?"

"They're fine," she said. "Guess what. I'm planning to open a Chinese restaurant at my café."

"A Chinese restaurant? Does Chavo know how to cook Chinese?"

"No. I have a Chinese partner."

"That's cool. Is he your boyfriend?"

Margo laughed. "He has a wife and two children."

"When do you plan to open this restaurant?"

"In about six weeks, if all goes well."

"Oh, I'm sorry. I'll be away at that time."

"Where are you going?" she asked, though she had already heard about the trip from Lindsey.

"I'm going to Mexico."

"With Diego?"

"Yeah. He's going to show me his country. We're going to Mexico City first, and then we're going to his family's ranch."

"His family has a ranch?"

"Of course. They've had it since the Spanish came there five hundred years ago."

That would explain why Diego looked European, but she was still skeptical. As impressive as Tricia's boyfriends sounded, they always turned out to have some flaw. "Where's the ranch?"

"It's northwest of Mexico City, an hour's drive."

"Well, how long do you plan to be away?"

"At least a month."

"So you quit your job?"

"Oh, yeah. I got tired of it."

Tricia always got tired of her jobs as well as tired of her boyfriends. "Are you keeping your apartment in Tarrytown?"

"Yeah. I'll find another job there after I get back."

Tricia always found another job, though she was unemployed during covid and she lived on payments from the government. "You know, I've heard some bad things about Mexico. I mean, about the gangs. So I hope you'll be safe there."

"Don't worry. Mexico City's as safe as New York City, and his family's ranch has an army to protect it."

"An army?" This was unsettling.

"It's not really an army, it's security guards."

"Why do they need security guards?"

"For the same reason that rich people need them here," Tricia explained. "To protect their property."

"Well, I don't want anything to happen to you," Margo said, mindful of the kidnappings and murders she had heard about in the news.

"Don't worry," Tricia assured her. "The bad shit only happens to tourists who don't know what to do in a foreign country. I'll be with a Mexican who knows what to do in his own country, so nothing's going to happen to me."

"Well, be careful. And please stay in touch."

"I will. I'll text you pictures."

After they ended the call she remained on the sofa where she had sat down at the beginning of their conversation, and she thought about Tricia, her last baby, the one that Jack had hoped would be a boy. But Tricia wasn't even a tomboy, she was very much a girl from day one, and as she grew up she became increasingly obsessed with her appearance. She would change her hairstyle more than once in the same day as if she was always seeking perfection and never finding it. She did the same thing with her jobs and her boyfriends, and she was evidently doing it now with Diego, pursuing something unattainable. Margo wondered if she would ever settle for reality, stick with a job, and stay with a boyfriend. She was almost thirty-four now, and before she knew it she might run out of time to have children.

The next morning she called Anthony and arranged to meet with him that afternoon. She didn't have to go straight home after closing the café because Keira was going to Lisa's house after school that day.

She had put the CLOSED sign on the door, and when he appeared precisely on time she let him in. He had brought a menu from the restaurant where he worked, and when they sat down at a table he showed it to her, indicating the dishes that were ordered most often. He didn't propose replicating their whole menu but selecting the most popular dishes for his menu. And the more he explained his vision for the business, the more she believed in it.

She explained Greta's idea of running the restaurant and the café as separate businesses, with him subletting from her, paying half the rent and utilities, and he agreed to this arrangement. The only major issue was the cost of starting up the restaurant, for which he had prepared a budget. He offered to pay the startup cost with money he had brought from Hong Kong, and his willingness to risk his own money, which he must have needed for other purposes, confirmed her trust in him.

After their meeting she called Robert, who was in his office because it was Thursday. When he heard what she wanted to talk about he suggested that she come and meet with him now. It was only a short walk on Warburton and then down Spring Street, so she arrived at his office within ten minutes. Robert, who no longer had a receptionist, greeted her at the front door and led her into a dimly lit room, which had photographs of sailboats on the walls. He invited her to sit on a sofa while he settled into an armchair. His hair was white, and his skin was tanned and wrinkled by the sun, but his eyes were as keen as ever. He asked her about her family, and then he asked her what she was up to. She explained what she and Anthony had agreed to, and then she began to field his questions.

"Does Anthony have legal status?"

"No. He's seeking asylum as a refugee from Hong Kong."

"Why did he leave Hong Kong?"

"To avoid going to prison."

"Would he go to prison if he went back there?"

"Yeah, for sure," she said. "So he should be entitled to asylum, shouldn't he?"

"He should be," Robert agreed. "But it'll take a while for him to be granted asylum, and in the meantime he can't be employed legally."

"He wouldn't be employed, he'd be the owner of a business."

"Is he going to invest money in this business?"

"He's going to pay the startup costs."

"Then there might not be a problem, but he needs a legal entity for the business, and with his status he can't create one." Robert paused. "But you have a legal entity, and you have a license to operate a restaurant, so you could use your company for that purpose."

"You mean there would be two businesses in the same company?"

"It would be one business, with different menus for the café and the restaurant. A lot of restaurants have different menus for different times of day."

"So how would we keep our activities separate?"

"You'd have separate sets of books. Greta can handle that."

"But what if his restaurant loses money?"

"Most restaurants lose money during their startup period. Does he have money to cover those losses?"

"I don't know. I believe he does."

"Well, if he doesn't, then his restaurant won't survive. But you'll still have your café."

"Yeah. But I'll be stuck with double the rent."

Robert studied her. "How well do you know this man?"

"I don't know him well," she admitted, "but for some reason I trust him. I can't explain, it's just a feeling."

"A good feeling?"

"Yeah, I guess. And at this point I don't have much choice. I mean, if I don't do this, I'll probably have to sell my house, and where will we live?"

"Where will all the people live who can't afford to stay in their houses?"

"That's a good question."

"At least if I had to sell my house, I could live on my boat."

"But what about the winter?"

"I'd take it to Florida."

She knew he was divorced, and his kids were grown up, and he loved his boat, so she could imagine him living on it. She thought for a while, and then she said: "Well, I'm going to do it. I'm going to bet on Anthony."

"And I'm going to pray for you," Robert said, smiling.

Two days later she met with Richard Pierce and proposed that she renew her lease for one year at double the rent, with an option to renew for four years. He tried to increase the rent for the renewal period, but she argued that if she had renewed for five years there wouldn't have been any further increase. He pointed out that by renewing now for only one year she was getting a concession, but she countered that she was sparing him the cost of finding a new tenant as well as the risk of having an empty space with no income, so he finally agreed not to increase the rent any further for the renewal period.

She checked with a friend who worked in the village's building department and was relieved to learn that her existing permit allowed her to operate a restaurant for dinner, so Anthony could go ahead and buy the woks, the rice cooker, and the utensils needed for Chinese food, and he could also hire the chef, whom he found in Flushing. The chef, whose name was Peter, had come from Hong Kong several years ago, and he was working as a sous chef at a Chinese restaurant on Central Avenue, so he was happy to advance to a higher level.

They discussed whether to get new tables and chairs for the restaurant, but to save money they agreed to cover the existing tables with linen in the evening to create an upscale ambience.

That Sunday was Mother's Day, and after Mass she stopped at the flower shop and bought a bouquet of mixed flowers to take to the cemetery for her mother's grave. Lindsey had good memories of her grandmother, who had recognized her mental ability, and though Keira was born after her great-grandmother died she had heard good things about her from Lindsey, so they were willing to accompany Margo.

The cemetery was right across the border of Yonkers so it didn't take them long to get there. Margo parked on the street that adjoined the cemetery, opened the trunk of her car, and took out a green plastic cone. They stopped at the faucet, just inside the cemetery, so she could fill the cone with water, and then they proceeded to the family plot, which her parents had purchased with foresight many years ago.

After passing a row of headstones with mostly Irish, Italian, and Polish names they came to her family's headstone. Her mother's and her father's names and dates were engraved on the left side, and her husband's name and dates were on the right, with a blank space for her. She knelt in front of where her mother's name was carved in the stone, Luisa Collins 1924 – 2009, and she pushed the spike of the cone into the soil. Lindsey handed her the flowers, which she arranged in the cone. With her eyes closed she recalled her earliest memory of her mother when they lived in the house where she lived now. At the time she was almost three, and she remembered her mother holding the baby she had just brought home from the hospital. Though Margo realized that she would no longer be the center of attention as she had been as the only child, somehow her mother assured her that she would be loved as much as before, and even after two more children were added to the family she found that her mother had more than enough love for all of them. And she said a prayer of thanks for her mother.

She rose to her feet and she gazed at the name of her husband, Jack Walsh 1949 – 2017, thinking about how she would lie beside him someday, as she had lain beside him for the thirty-five years of their marriage, and then she murmured a prayer for him.

"I miss him," Lindsey said.

"I do too," Keira said.

She put an arm around each one of them appreciatively. "He was a good man, and he loved you so much."

On the following Wednesday the restaurant had its grand opening. In the absence of a local newspaper they announced the opening on social media, and they strung flags over the sidewalk in front of the café. The first night they had only five customers, but every day as the word got around they had more customers, and by their third week they had to take reservations for tables. It helped that they were getting excellent reviews on the website that Anthony had commissioned, and that they were having a steady flow of Chinese customers, which other customers noted as a favorable sign. So everything was going well on the evening when, as she was sitting in the kitchen at home, playing checkers with her granddaughter, she got a phone call from the U.S. embassy in Mexico City.

FIVE

After verifying that she was the mother of Patricia Walsh the woman on the phone informed her that her daughter had an accident and was in the hospital.

"Oh, my God," Margo said. "What happened to her?"

"I can't give you all the details, but I can tell you she was wounded in her leg by a gunshot."

"A gunshot?"

"Yes. She's had surgery," the woman told her, "and she's doing well, but it'll take a while for her to recover, and she'll need someone to accompany her on the flight home."

"How long will it take for her to recover?"

"If you talk to the doctor, he can tell you. I'll give you his phone number."

"Does he speak English?"

"Oh, yes. He did his residency at a hospital in Austin, Texas."

She picked up a pen and the notepad from the counter, and she wrote down the doctor's name and phone number.

"If you need help in making arrangements, I'd be happy to help you," the woman offered, and then she gave Margo her name and phone number.

"Okay. Thanks."

They ended the call, and Margo took a long deep breath.

"What was that about?" Keira asked her.

"Your Aunt Tricia had an accident."

"She did?" Keira said with concern. "Where?"

"In Mexico City. That call was from the U.S. embassy there."

"What happened to Aunt Tricia?"

She hesitated but then decided to tell Keira: "She was wounded in her leg by a gunshot."

"She was? Who shot her?"

"I don't know. But she's in the hospital, and she's doing well, thank God."

After a sober pause Keira said: "You were worried about her going to Mexico."

"Yeah, I was." And she wondered if the shooting had anything to do with her boyfriend.

"Are you gonna go to Mexico?" Keira asked her.

"I don't know. Before I do anything, I'm going to talk with the doctor who's treating her." She didn't know what time it was in Mexico City, but she guessed it was at least two hours earlier, so it would be two in the afternoon there. And hoping the doctor was in his office, she called the number that the woman at the embassy had given her.

"Hola?" a woman answered. *"La oficina del Dr. Pérez."*

"Do you speak English?" Margo asked her.

"Yes, a little."

"Well, I am the mother of Patricia Walsh," she said slowly, "a patient of the doctor. Could I please speak with him?"

"I will find him."

She waited apprehensively.

"This is Dr. Pérez," a man said. "Are you Mrs. Walsh?"

"Yes," she said. "Can you tell me how my daughter's doing?"

"She's doing well. She was wounded in the right thigh, but luckily the bullet didn't hit the bone or an artery, and the surgery was successful."

"How long will it take for her to recover?"

"She should stay in the hospital for about a week. And then she will need someone to accompany her on the flight home."

"Okay," she said. "Do you know where it happened?"

"I only know what the police told us. And they didn't tell us very much. They only said she was in a bar with her boyfriend."

"Did he get shot?"

The doctor paused, and then he said: "He got shot in the face and in the chest, and he was dead when the police arrived."

"My God. So someone wanted to kill him."

"Evidently. The police said he was the likely target, and your daughter was hit accidentally."

"Were gangs involved?"

"The police didn't say. But gangs are usually involved in these things."

Remembering her suspicions, she asked: "Did the police say anything about the boyfriend?"

"They said he was on their wanted list for drug trafficking."

"Then how did he get back into your country?"

"It wouldn't have been a problem," the doctor said. "He only had to tip the immigration officer."

"Is that how it works there?"

"That's how it works everywhere."

"Well, I'll have to figure out what to do. I don't want to leave my daughter alone in the hospital."

"It would speed her recovery to have a family member with her. And there's a good hotel nearby where you could stay."

"Does she have a phone in her room?"

"No, but you can ask them to provide one. I'll give you a number you can call." He paused, and then he gave her a number.

She had just ended the call when Lindsey came home, as usual looking wiped out, and she must have sensed something in the air because she asked: "What's happening?"

"Aunt Tricia got shot," Keira informed her.

"What?" Lindsey said. "What are you talking about?"

"She was wounded in the right thigh," Margo said. "But she had surgery, and she's doing well."

"Where the hell is she?"

"In Mexico, where she went with her boyfriend. Remember?"

"Yeah, but I didn't know she was still there."

"She's still there, and she'll be there for a while longer."

"Oh, man," Lindsey groaned. "What kind of shit did she get herself into?"

"From what the doctor told me, it was her boyfriend's shit."

"I never met him, but I didn't like the sound of him. Did she get shot on his family's ranch?"

"It happened in a bar in Mexico City. The doctor said he was the likely target, and Tricia was hit accidentally."

"Was her boyfriend killed?"

"Yeah," Margo said. "But I don't want to talk about him. I want to talk about Tricia."

Lindsey opened the refrigerator and took out a bottle of wine. "How long will she be in the hospital?"

"The doctor said she should stay there for about a week."

"Then someone should go there and be with her."

"Yeah, I agree. And I should go."

"Could you be away from your business now?" Lindsey asked her, pouring an almost full glass of wine.

"Well, I'd have Chavo in the kitchen, but I'd need someone to mind the front."

"Maybe you could ask your partner to do that."

"Maybe I could, but it's a lot to ask. He'd have to be there from eight in the morning until ten at night."

"That's only twelve hours. Nurses work that long."

"I know, but it's still a lot to ask."

After a silence, during which she appeared to be thinking, Lindsey asked: "Do you have a passport?"

"Oh, yeah. I got it several years ago."

"How many years ago?"

"I don't know." And then she remembered. "I got it for the trip to Ireland with your dad, the year before you got married."

"Well, that was more than ten years go, so your passport has expired."

"Shit. How long does it take to renew a passport?"

"I'll see," Lindsey said, taking out her phone. She typed some things, and then she said: "Two to three weeks."

"By then she'll be out of the hospital. And someone will have to be with her on the flight home."

"So call Shannon. Maybe she could go."

Already having had that idea, Margo picked up the landline phone and punched in the number of her oldest daughter.

Shannon answered after two rings.

Margo explained the situation and then said: "I'd go myself, but my passport has expired, and it takes two to three weeks to renew a passport. So could you go?"

"How long would I have to be there?"

"For about a week."

After a silence Shannon said: "I couldn't be away that long. But I could go and be with her on the flight home."

"That would help. But I don't want her to be alone for a week in a Mexican hospital."

"Do you have a phone number for her?"

"No, but when I have one I'll give it to you."

"The poor thing," Shannon said. "I wouldn't want to be in her situation."

"I wouldn't either. I hope she'll learn from this experience."

"I'll pray for her. And let me know if you want me to go and bring her home. Okay?"

"Okay." She ended the call, blaming herself for not taking a stronger stand against Tricia's trip to Mexico, though she knew she couldn't have stopped her.

"So she can't go," Lindsey said.

"No, she can't be away that long."

"If I was older," Keira said, "I'd go."

"I know you would," Margo said. "You're a good girl."

"You know," Lindsey said after a long silence, "I have two weeks of vacation coming, so I could go."

"Do you have a passport?"

Lindsey nodded. "I got one for our trip to Punta Cana, and that was only eight years ago, so it hasn't expired."

"Can I go with you?" Keira asked her.

"Not on this trip. You can go on the next one."

"You really want to go?" Margo said, taken by surprise. Her two younger daughters had never been the best of friends.

"Yeah, I do. It would help you, and it would give me a chance to think about my life."

"Okay. Thank you." She moved around the counter and put her arm around Lindsey and hugged her.

After getting a glass of wine for herself she called the number that Dr. Pérez had given her and arranged to get a phone for Tricia. Then she called Shannon to let her know that Lindsey was going to Mexico. And finally, while Lindsey used her phone to schedule a flight, she began making dinner.

On Saturday, as people were having breakfast at her café, she got a call from the hospital from a woman who gave her the number of the phone they had installed in Tricia's room, and standing at the counter she called the number at her first opportunity.

After several rings a weak voice said: "Hello?"

"Hi, Tricia. It's Mom."

"Where are you?"

"I'm at the café. How do you feel?"

"Like shit," Tricia said. "They give me pills for the pain, but it only helps for a little while."

"Do you have a lot of pain now?"

"No. But I will after this pill wears off."

"I talked with the doctor yesterday," Margo said, "and he told me you're doing well."

"Yeah, that's what he told me, but I don't see how I'll ever walk again."

"You will. But you'll probably need physical therapy."

"I can't wait."

"Well, guess what. Lindsey's flying to Mexico tomorrow, and she'll be there with you until you come home."

"Lindsey? You're not coming?"

"I can't. My passport has expired, and it takes two to three weeks to renew a passport. By then you'll be home."

"I hope I will."

"So how's the food?"

"It sucks. It's not Mexican food, it's hospital food."

"But you should eat it. You need sustenance."

"Yeah, I will. But I wish they'd give me tacos or tamales."

"Just eat whatever they give you. Okay?"

"Okay. I gotta get off the phone now. A nurse wants to check my bandage."

"We can talk later. I love you."

"I love you too."

She stood there for a while imagining her youngest daughter lying in a hospital bed in a foreign country. She wished she could be there to comfort her and speed her recovery. But she could only pray for her.

Lindsey's flight was in the morning, and since Margo had never driven to the airport instead of paying for a taxi she got Shannon to drive them there, which Shannon did gladly. Shannon also offered to pay for Lindsey's trip, but Margo thanked her and told her to save the money for another occasion.

That afternoon she was relieved to hear from Lindsey that she had arrived safely and planned to visit Tricia at the hospital in the evening. Margo was having dinner with Keira when they called her, alternating on the phone, and she was thankful that they were getting along so well. At least there was something good about this family emergency—it had given Lindsey and Tricia an opportunity to develop a new relationship.

After putting Keira to bed she went out to the front porch with a glass of wine and sat there recovering from the excitement of the day. The house across the street was dark as usual, and there was no activity on the street.

Then out of the shadows a figure emerged, walking up her sidewalk. As he came into the light from the porch she saw it was a young man, and she had no idea who he was until he said: "Hello, Mrs. Walsh. I'm Dylan."

"Dylan?" He was a playmate of Tricia who lived in one of the larger houses toward Broadway on the other side of the street. His parents had adopted him and his sister as orphans of the war in Guatemala. At the time he was three, the same age as Tricia, and they started playing together when they were around five.

Since he remained standing on the sidewalk she said: "Come and join me."

As he climbed the steps she noticed that he looked pretty much the same as the last time she had seen him, which must have been about ten years ago, the year when his parents sold their house and retired to Florida.

"I'm glad to see you," he said, approaching her.

"Come and sit down. Would you like a glass of wine?"

"Oh, no, thanks." He sat down and gazed at her with his look of a lost little boy that she remembered.

"What brings you to Hastings?"

"I had dinner tonight with my sister in Sleepy Hollow, and I thought I'd stop here on my way back to the city."

The last she knew he lived in LA, and she waited for him to explain what he was doing in New York.

"I'm here for a week in a training program."

"What kind of program?"

"For counselors," he said. "I work for a nonprofit organization as a counselor for young people who have drug problems."

Since he had struggled with a drug problem for many years she could see how he might be good in this position. "Do you like being a counselor?"

"Oh, yeah. It's the most rewarding thing I've ever done."

"Where do you work?"

"I work in a neighborhood that's mostly Latinos, so I feel at home there."

She remembered how with his straight black hair, his dark eyes, and his brown skin he hadn't felt at home in Hastings. Through his childhood and adolescence Tricia had been his only friend. "So how's your Spanish?"

"It was hard learning it as a second language, but I finally speak it well. Though the kids tell me I still have a gringo accent."

"How's your sister?"

"She's doing fine. She's a teacher at an elementary school in Sleepy Hollow, and she's married now with two children."

Since their mother had been a teacher at the elementary school in Dobbs Ferry she said: "Your mom must be proud of her."

"Yeah. Mom always hoped she'd become a teacher. And of course Dad always hoped I'd become a lawyer."

Instead of going to college Dylan left Hastings after graduating from high school and went to LA with the hope of getting into the movies. As a teenager he had loved the movies, and almost every Saturday during high school he and Tricia had taken a Beeline bus to a multiplex in Elmsford and spent the day bingeing on movies. For a while he got bit parts in movies playing Latinos, but then that work dried up.

"So where's Tricia?" he finally asked.

"Oh," she sighed. "Poor Tricia."

"What happened to her?"

Without pausing to take a breath she poured out: "She went to Mexico with her boyfriend, and he took her to a bar where he got killed and she got wounded."

"Oh, my God," he said with concern. "How badly wounded?"

"She got shot in her leg, and she's in a hospital in Mexico City. But she's going to be all right."

"Thank God. Do you have a phone number for her?"

"Yeah. I'll give it to you." She got out her phone and found the number, which he put into his own phone. "She'd be glad to hear from you."

"Thanks. Who was this boyfriend?"

"He was a guy who pretended to be a wealthy Mexican from an old family but turned out to be a drug dealer."

"I feel bad for her," he said softly. "You know, of all the people I've known in my life, Tricia was the best. For me she was a life saver."

They talked for a while longer, and then he left to catch a train into the city. As she watched him ambling down the street she was thankful that he had dropped by. It made her feel better about her wayward youngest daughter.

She talked every day with Tricia at the hospital, with Lindsey at the hotel, and with both of them together. Tricia happily informed her that Lindsey was smuggling food into the hospital, and that she was enjoying the best tacos, tamales, and enchiladas she ever had. From their conversations Margo learned that Lindsey was using her free time during the day to visit the historical sights of Mexico City, including the Zócalo, the Cathedral, the Palace of Fine Arts, the National Museum of Anthropology, Chapultepec Castle, the Basilica of Our Lady of Guadalupe, and the Frida Kahlo Museum. Her favorite was the Anthropology Museum, which she visited several times. She said she would have gone to Mass at the Cathedral, but it was all in Spanish, so she wouldn't have understood a word of it.

After the phone conversations with her daughters Margo spent the evenings watching television with Keira, who introduced her to the programs she watched with her mother. They were mostly sit-coms about families so Margo had no problem with them except for the commercials. It seemed that almost half the viewing time was devoted to commercials, and not only that but most of the commercials promoted drugs for a spectrum of maladies, ranging from vaginal odor to depression. As she remembered, they didn't use to promote drugs on television, maybe because of legal restrictions, but now they had an open field. And what were people expected to do? Go to their doctors and demand the drugs they had heard about from these commercials? Was that how the healthcare system was supposed to work? And wasn't it fraudulent for the commercials to promote the benefits of the drugs in clear loud voices but only mumble the side effects in barely audible, rapid strings of words, which no one could possibly understand? After an evening of being bombarded by commercials Margo insisted on having the remote so that she could press the mute button at the first sign of an impending commercial, which most people probably did. And after putting Keira to bed she went back to the programs she usually watched on public television and streaming services.

One evening when she turned on the television nothing happened. The screen was blank, and at first she thought the power cord might have come unplugged. But it wasn't that. With

Keira's help she checked all the possibilities for what was wrong, which included replacing the batteries in the remote and rebooting the service. But still nothing happened. They finally concluded that the television set had died. In fact, she and Jack had bought this set almost seventeen years ago when it was the latest model. The store where they had bought it had gone out of business, so she called Shannon and got a recommendation for where to buy a new one. Since she didn't have the time to go to this store, which was over on Central Avenue, they found it online, and after a half hour chat with a person or a robot they decided to buy a new model of the same brand. The only problem, other than the price, was that the current models all had much larger screen sizes than the one they had. They chose the smallest of these sizes, and they were assured by the person or the robot that the set had a pedestal so that it could be placed on the table they had. But when the guy from the store delivered it two days later they found that it didn't have a pedestal, it had legs at both ends, so it barely fit on the table. Since it looked unstable Margo ordered a larger table online, which you had to assemble yourself, and since her skills didn't include assembling furniture she called Patrick and got him to do it. Of course if Jack had still been around he could have done it easily. It took Patrick about two hours to put the table together, and there they were with a new television projecting almost life-sized people into the family room.

All went well until two days later when Keira turned on the television and there was no sound. They went through all the trouble-shooting procedures in the manual until Keira discovered that there was no sound because someone or something had turned the volume down to zero. In the end they decided it must have happened due to the confusion of their now having three remotes: one for the set, another for the cable TV, and another for streaming. It seemed that everything in the high-tech world kept getting more and more complicated.

On Monday when things had quieted after lunch she joined Greta at the usual table. Greta complimented the food with only a minor suggestion for improvement, and then she asked: "Have you heard about the proposed bond issue?"

"No, I haven't," Margo said. Without the local newspaper it was hard to keep up on things, and she had been preoccupied with Tricia's situation. "What are they proposing?"

"They're proposing an issue of $62.3 million for projects at the school."

"Didn't we just have a bond issue for projects at the school?"

"We did—only four years ago. For $18 million."

"So what do they want to do now?"

"It looks like they want to add two wings to the main building for classrooms, breakout rooms, resource rooms, offices, and a new cafeteria. They also want to revamp the athletic fields with artificial turf."

"Artificial turf? What's wrong with grass?"

"It needs to be watered and cut."

"But why do they need additional rooms? The enrollment's about the same as it was when we went to school."

"It's actually lower."

"Then what's the purpose?"

"The purpose is to have a school like they have in Scarsdale," Greta said caustically.

"Well, if people want a school like they have in Scarsdale, they should go and live in Scarsdale."

"Yeah, they should. They shouldn't live here."

Bracing herself, Margo asked: "So how much would this bond issue increase our taxes?"

"From what I hear, it would increase them for the average taxpayer by about fifteen hundred dollars."

"Shit. That's going to hurt a lot of people."

"It's especially going to hurt people who are sixty-five and over living mainly on Social Security, which is more than a fifth of the residents of this village. But the members of the school board either don't know that, or they don't care. They want a school like they have in Scarsdale while their kids are in school, and then they'll sell their houses for even more than they paid for them and move to Florida or Arizona."

"Leaving us with higher taxes."

"Well, they have to put this proposal to a referendum."

"But the last proposal was approved."

"This one's a lot higher. In fact, it's more than three times as much. And we *have* turned down proposals before."

"Yeah, I know," Margo muttered. "And what the hell is a resource room?"

"I don't know. I guess it's a room where they keep resources."

"But we didn't have them when we were in school, and our children didn't have them. So why do they need them?"

"Why do they need all those things they spend money on?"

It was a good question. It went right to the heart of what was happening to the village where they had grown up.

As the time approached for her return Tricia made a few decisions. She was living in a one-bedroom apartment in Tarrytown on the second floor of an old building above a restaurant, and since she avoided making commitments she didn't have a lease for a fixed period, she only rented by the month. Also, since the apartment was furnished she could leave without having to take anything with her except for her clothes and her personal items. So her first decision was to move out of her apartment, and with Margo's encouragement her second decision was to come back home, at least until she recovered from her wound.

She had to give notice to her landlord, which she did by phone, and Margo had to remove her belongings from the apartment, which she did the following afternoon with the help of Keira. The landlord met her in front of the building, and after he led her up the stairs and let her into the apartment he agreed that Tricia didn't owe him any more money because she had paid in advance for the month of June.

It took her and Keira a number of trips up and down the stairs to remove all of Tricia's belongings and put them into the trunk and the back seat of her car, which was parked in a space that the landlord had saved for her. And when they got home, since they were tired from going up and down stairs, they decided to leave Tricia's things in the car until the next day.

Margo then had to decide where to put Tricia in her house. She could have her share a bedroom with Lindsey, but that hadn't worked when they were growing up, and to put them back together now might destroy the new relationship they were developing in Mexico. She could move Keira back into her mother's bedroom, but that would feel like a setback for Keira, and it would prolong her separation from her mother. So she would have to put Tricia into the bedroom she was using as an office, and that would mean relocating her office. The only place where it could go was on the third floor, which had been an attic when her parents bought the house. To create a place where their children could play they covered the studs with drywall, laid a wall-to-wall carpet on the rough wooden floor, and installed electrical outlets. So when they were children Margo and Colleen and Audrey and Patrick spent most of their time at home on the third floor, playing games and doing projects and quarreling.

Margo's children also spent most of their time there but after they left home the third floor reverted to an attic, a place where they could store things they might need again, including a cane, a pair of crutches, a walker, and a wheelchair, or things they kept for sentimental reasons, including books they might read again and photo albums that went back to the time of her grandparents. Instead of being piled on the floor the books and albums were in bookcases that Jack had built to hold them. Margo hadn't gone up to the third floor in quite a while, and now as she approached a bookcase she saw that the books and the albums were gathering dust. She took out the photo album of her parents' wedding, and she carefully opened it. There were photos of the outside and the inside of Our Lady of Mt. Carmel where they had the wedding Mass, and there were photos of the Italian restaurant on Yonkers Avenue where they had the reception. There were posed photos of the bride and groom alone, of the bride and groom with the wedding party, the bride with her family, the groom with his family, and candid photos of Italians and Irish at the reception, eating and drinking and celebrating. The photos were in color, but after more than seventy years they were faded, especially the blues, but the faces of her mother and father still glowed with joy. And Margo was touched by how young they looked.

Reflecting, she believed that her parents had a happy marriage, though on their wedding day they had no idea of the challenges they would face, just as on their wedding day she and Jack had no idea of the challenges they would face. For both marriages she thought the greatest challenges were the children, followed by economic and health problems. It took faith, hope, and love to be married and to continue being married.

She closed the album and returned it to its place in the bookcase, and she looked around, deciding to locate her office near the dormer window that faced the woods beyond the aqueduct. But she had to get a desk, a chair, and two file cabinets up the stairs to the third floor, and since there weren't any guys in the house she called a longtime friend whose landscaping business she used, and she asked him if he could get two of his guys to haul her furniture upstairs. They were there the next afternoon, two solid guys who performed the task with no trouble. As she tipped them she mentioned that two of her daughters were in Mexico City, and they said they had always wanted to visit the capital of their country but never had. When they were gone she sat at her desk, and she could see the advantage of having her office on the third floor: if people wanted to talk with her they would have to climb all those stairs.

Next she had to get a bed for Tricia, so she and Keira went to a used furniture store in Yonkers where she found a bed, a chair, and a chest of drawers, to be delivered. Then on the phone she ordered a new mattress with box springs as well as two sets of sheets from a chain furniture store in Elmsford. And finally she ordered a window air conditioner from the store where she had bought the units for the bedrooms.

She charged all these purchases to her credit card, knowing she would have other extra expenses on her card that month but hoping that somehow she could pay the balance when it was due. Of course she could always pay in instalments but with the interest rates they charged it was better to give up eating than to finance the balance of a credit card.

The day before Lindsey and Tricia were scheduled to fly home she sat at a table with Anthony after closing the café. She didn't have to leave right away because Keira was with Lisa at the village pool.

Anthony talked about the restaurant for a while, and then he asked: "Is the church open now?"

"Which church?"

"St. Matthew."

"Are you a Catholic?"

He nodded. He reached inside his shirt and pulled up a wooden cross at the end of the cord around his neck and showed it to her, saying: "This is made of olive wood from Bethlehem."

She recognized it, having seen crosses like it. Impressed, she could only think of asking: "Are there many Catholics in Hong Kong?"

"Oh, yeah. There used to be more, but there are still about four hundred thousand."

"How does the government feel about Catholics?"

"They don't like us. In fact, being Catholic makes things worse for me. It could get me an extra year or two in prison."

"Are priests involved in the opposition?"

"A few of them are, but most of them aren't. They don't want to attract attention to their parishes."

"What about the few?"

"One was arrested and sent to prison."

"For being a priest?"

"No. For expressing his opinion. But it didn't help that he was a priest."

"Were you raised as a Catholic?"

"Yeah. I went to St. Anthony's School, and my family went to St. Anthony's Church."

"Then you were named for St. Anthony."

"St. Anthony of Padua. Today's his feast day."

She should have known this because her mother had always observed that day, her family having come from Italy. "So where do you go to Mass here?"

"St. Brigid in Yonkers, which is near where I live."

"Well, St. Matthew is open now."

"Good." He pushed back his chair. "I'll go over and light a candle. How much are the candles?"

"As much as you want to donate, but at least a dollar."

"I'll be back soon."

She watched him walk out and turn left and head north. The revelation that he was a Catholic made her feel closer to him.

The flight from Mexico arrived in the late afternoon, so Keira went with her to the airport, driven by Shannon. With all the construction it was chaotic at the airport, and it took them a while to get to where they could pick up Lindsey and Tricia. In fact, it wasn't possible for them to pull over to the curb, so they stopped one row out from the curb despite an official yelling at them to move on, and Keira jumped out and helped get her aunt and the luggage into the car. Glancing back at them from the front seat, Margo noticed that Tricia looked drained while Lindsey seemed energized by her trip.

On the way home at least two of them talked at the same time, skipping from one topic to another but mainly recounting all that had happened during the past ten days, and when they got home Keira helped bring in the luggage while Shannon helped Tricia walking with a cane surmount the five wooden steps to the porch, where she sank heavily into a chair, saying she needed to rest before she went into the house.

Margo wondered if she should have put the bed in the living room so Tricia wouldn't have to climb stairs, but after resting for a while Tricia got up and entered the house and holding on to the banister gamely started up the stairs, saying: "Up with the good and down with the bad."

"That's what the therapist told her," Lindsey said.

"In English?" Margo asked.

"No, in Spanish. They told her '*Arriba lo bueno y abajo lo malo*,' but we figured out what it meant."

"I'll have to remember that. I mean, if I ever break a leg in Mexico."

"The nurse said a lot of tourists break legs," Lindsey said as they followed Tricia up the stairs.

"They do?"

"Yeah. She said they don't watch where they're going."

They followed Tricia into the bedroom.

"Do you like it?" Margo asked her.

"I love it," Tricia said, turning and facing her. She had tears in her eyes. "Oh, Mom, I've been so stupid."

Margo went to her and hugged her, saying: "We should just be thankful that you're all right."

Tricia nodded, with her wet cheeks rubbing against Margo's. "Yeah, I know how lucky I am. I could have been killed."

"We can talk about that later. Right now why don't you lie down and try out your new bed."

"The bed isn't new," Keira pointed out. "But the mattress is."

Tricia lay down with her head on the pillow. "Yeah, this is better than the hospital bed."

"So rest for a while," Margo told her. "And then we'll have dinner."

"Okay," Tricia said, closing her eyes.

They left her and went down to the kitchen, where Lindsey got a bottle of wine out of the refrigerator and Margo got out the dinner she had prepared in advance. It was chili with ground beef and kidney beans, so all she had to do was put it on the stove and cook the rice.

Since there were four of them, and since this was a special occasion, they ate at the dining room table with Tricia at the end nearest to the kitchen.

Lindsey, sitting across the table from her daughter, looked happy for a change.

"Did you have a good trip?" Margo asked her.

"I had a great trip," Lindsey said. "It was good for me to get away and spend time in another world."

"Get away from what?" Keira asked her.

"Not away from you, or from Mom, but away from that damn hospital. It gave me a chance to think about my life."

"So did you make any decisions?" Margo asked her.

"Yeah. I did. I decided to look for another job, and I decided to go back for a master's degree."

"I think those are very good decisions."

"Remember how I didn't believe I could still get a master's degree? Well, now I believe I can," Lindsey said with confidence.

"I know you can," Margo told her.

Margo had arranged with Anthony to manage the café the next day, which wouldn't be busy at breakfast time because it was Saturday, so she had the whole weekend to spend with her family. That morning Lindsey changed the bandage on Tricia's leg and applied antiseptic salve to the wound. She also made sure that Tricia kept taking the antibiotic pills she was supposed to take for another five days. They mostly spent the day sitting on the front porch, talking and getting used to being together again.

Though she was a professed atheist, Tricia joined them at Mass on Sunday, but she didn't take communion on the grounds that she hadn't gone to confession. It was Father's Day, and after lunch Margo planned to go to the cemetery in Yonkers. To her surprise Tricia wanted to go with her, so they went together. She had bought flowers for the occasion, red carnations, enough for both her father and her husband, and she took them out of the vase where she was keeping them, put them into a plastic bag, and helped Tricia through the front door and down the steps and over to the driveway.

"So you still have this car," Tricia said as she got into it.

"Oh, yeah. I don't plan to buy another one."

"How many miles does it have?"

"About eighty thousand."

"That's less than I have on my car."

"Where is it?" she asked as they edged out of the driveway.

"It's parked in my space behind the building."

"Mm. Well, that's strange. When I got your things from your apartment, the landlord didn't mention it."

"Maybe he wants to keep it," Tricia joked. "But he probably just forgot about it. He'll want that space for his new tenant."

"Then we should go and get it."

"I guess we should. Can we park it on your street?"

"We can if we get it today," she said as they headed toward Broadway. "All the other days of the week there wouldn't be a place for it because of the cars and trucks and vans of people working on the house across from me."

"How long ago did they buy that house?"

"Almost two years ago."

"And they're still working on it?"

"They're always working on it. They didn't buy the house to live in, they bought it to have a construction project."

It took them less than ten minutes to get to the cemetery. They parked on the street, she got two green plastic cones out of her trunk, and they entered by the main gate. There was a high step up from the interior road to the main level, which Margo carefully climbed before offering a hand to Tricia. The last thing either of them needed at this point was to fall and break a bone in the cemetery.

She handed the flowers to Tricia while she filled the cones with water from the faucet, and then she led Tricia across the cemetery, passing the large granite stones of people she had known or whose names she recognized from coming here over the years until they came to their family stone, where they stopped. After a moment of silence she knelt and pushed the spike of one cone into the ground in front of her father and then the spike of the other cone into the ground in front of her husband. She took the flowers from Tricia and arranged them in the cones, dividing them more or less equally. In the ground nearby were brass plates commemorating the war service of her father and her husband, and she brushed away some blades of grass from the plates that a mower must have thrown on them. Still on one knee she honored her father, who crossed an ocean to get to this country and found a job in a factory and served in the army and returned to his job and raised a family and lost his job and found a job as a bartender. Then she honored her husband, who served in the army and mastered the trade of being a plumber and helped so many people and was such a good father to his three daughters. And she gave thanks for having good men as her father and her husband.

As she glanced at Tricia, who was gazing at Jack's name on the stone, she believed that Tricia had the same feelings about him. They hadn't always gotten along, but no matter how often she disappointed him Jack was always there for her, and she must have known how much he loved her because she reached out and touched his name thankfully.

Since it was too soon in her healing process for Tricia to drive, Margo asked Lindsey to go with them and get Tricia's car, which they found where Tricia had left it. Tricia rode back with Lindsey, and they found a parking place on the street which wouldn't be available on Monday because of the vehicles from the endless construction project. They could have squeezed the car into the driveway along with Margo's and Lindsey's cars, but with three cars in the driveway they would usually have to move another car for someone to get her car out, and anyway Margo wanted to establish her right to at least one parking place on the street.

That night, as she lay in bed before going to sleep, she felt that things were going well. The two daughters who lived with her now were getting along, and for once she wasn't worrying about Tricia, who at least until her leg healed had a limited scope for getting into trouble. And she slept better than she had for a while.

SIX

ON MONDAY SHE called her doctor to get a recommendation for a specialist to check Tricia's wound. Her doctor, an immigrant from Croatia, had an office on Main Street, so Margo could easily walk there. She saw her doctor every six months to get a checkup and a prescription to renew her medication for blood pressure. Her doctor was affiliated with St. John's Riverside Hospital in Yonkers, and she recommended a colleague there. Margo called the specialist, whose name sounded Indian, and she made an appointment for Thursday.

The next day they had the beginning of a heat wave, the worst that Margo could remember, and she was really glad she had installed an air conditioner on the third floor because without it she couldn't have worked in her office. For most of the time they had lived in the house they didn't need air conditioning because of the breezes from the river, but with global warming the summers got hotter, and fans in the bedrooms couldn't keep them cool enough for sleeping, so reluctantly they installed air conditioners in the windows. While they gained in physical comfort, they lost in mental comfort from the sounds of the night they no longer heard: the rustling of leaves, the hum of a barge out on the river, the rumbling of a freight train.

Even after installing air conditioners in the bedrooms they still didn't have them on the main floor, but three years ago Margo addressed the problem of the kitchen which because it had windows on two walls and a door on a third wall was uncomfortably hot during the summer and uncomfortably cold during the winter. At the suggestion of her brother, Patrick, she bought a mini split for the kitchen, with Patrick doing the electrical work and a guy he knew installing the unit, and it was the best home improvement she had ever done.

The heat affected her business at the café because some elderly people heeded warnings not to go outside during the day, and Margo felt bad for them, wondering if she should have a delivery service. School would be out for the summer after Friday, so teenage kids would be available for delivering food, and maybe she could hire a few of them. She decided to ask Greta what she thought about the idea. Unlike the elderly who were staying home Greta continued coming to the café for lunch, explaining half in jest that because she had ancestors from Sicily she had a genetic resistance to heat.

At lunchtime, as soon as she had an opportunity, Margo joined her friend at the corner table and asked: "How's the food?"

"It's good. I like this soup." It was asparagus and avocado, pureed and served cold.

"He's going to keep making cold soups until this heat wave ends."

"They say it won't end until early next week."

"I hope they're wrong."

"They're always wrong—except when you want them to be wrong. So how are things going with your family?"

"They're going well. Lindsey and Tricia are getting along. Tricia's going to see a specialist this Thursday, who should give her a prescription for physical therapy."

"How's she doing mentally?"

"She seems okay, but I usually can't tell what she's feeling. She keeps it to herself."

"Well, she must be suffering from the trauma of being with a guy who got shot and killed."

"Yeah, she must be, but she hasn't talked about it."

"You know, she could have post-traumatic stress disorder."

"Post-traumatic stress disorder?" She had heard about it, but she didn't know exactly what it was. "What's that?"

"It's a mental disorder that you can have after a traumatic experience, like what happened to our troops who served in Afghanistan and Iraq."

"You mean what my father called shell shock?"

"Yeah. I know about it because one of my nephews had it. He served in Afghanistan."

"What are the symptoms?"

"Thinking about what happened," Greta said, "reliving it, having nightmares about it, feeling severe anxiety."

"I haven't noticed those symptoms, but I haven't been looking for them. And maybe she should have mental therapy, but I think she wants to deal with her leg first."

"Okay. But keep an eye out for those symptoms."

"I will," she said. Then, changing the subject, she said: "I had an idea, and I want to know what you think about it."

"What's your idea?"

"Some elderly customers are staying home because of the heat. And I feel bad for them, so maybe I could deliver food to them."

"How would you do that?"

"Well, I could hire kids from the high school."

"Yeah. They're out for the summer after this Friday." Greta paused, thinking. "But the kids who'd want the job probably don't have cars, and the kids who have cars probably wouldn't want the job. So I don't know about hiring kids."

"Then I could use a delivery service."

"That would cost you more, but it would be more reliable. And maybe you could use one of those online services that delivers for restaurants."

"They take a percentage, don't they?"

"Oh, yeah. They want to make money."

"Well, I don't want to make money on the service."

"I understand. So how will you let your customers know you can deliver to them?"

"I'll do what I did during covid. I'll distribute fliers and post announcements on the internet."

"Yeah, that worked. If you put an announcement on our local Facebook page, people will see it. They go there to see pictures of their grandchildren."

"And I still have addresses of customers we delivered to during covid," she said, fleshing out her plan. "But I don't have addresses for new customers since then."

"You could get their addresses when they pick up food."

"Yeah. I just have to get through this heat wave."

"We all just have to get through it."

On Thursday the temperature was in the high nineties when she drove Tricia to Yonkers for her appointment with the specialist, whose office was in one of the medical buildings across from St. John's. Tricia had a disk with her MRI from the hospital in Mexico City which she handed to the young woman at the desk so the doctor could review it.

They found two empty chairs in the crowded waiting area. Most of the people were young men, but one was a boy with his arm in a sling who looked about ten years old. She wondered if he was the victim of a school shooting, but even though she frequently heard about shootings on the news she didn't remember one in their area, so he could be the victim of another kind of gun violence. She couldn't understand why the government allowed almost anyone to own a gun. Did the politicians benefit from gun violence?

About fifteen minutes later she heard a nurse call Tricia's name, and at Tricia's request she followed her daughter into the examination room. The nurse, a Latina, asked her to sit in a chair at one side of the room while Tricia removed her sweatpants and put on a hospital gown and sat on the examination table. After taking Tricia's vital signs the nurse told her the doctor would be with her shortly.

The doctor, who was probably in his mid-fifties, greeted them cheerfully in an Indian accent. He was tall and lean and good looking.

"How are you feeling?" he asked Tricia kindly.

"I'm feeling okay," Tricia said.

"Do you still have pain?"

"Yeah, but not as much as before."

"And you're still taking the antibiotics?"

"Oh, yeah. I haven't missed a single day of them."

"Good. You don't want to risk an infection. Is your digestion system coping with the antibiotics?"

"Yeah. I eat some yogurt every day."

At that point the nurse returned and removed the bandage so the doctor could examine the wound.

"It's healing nicely," he told her. "You had muscle damage, but the bullet didn't hit the bone or an artery. You're lucky."

"I know."

"I'm going to prescribe a month of physical therapy, twice a week, which should be enough. But if it's not, I can prescribe more. And be sure to change the bandage every day."

"They said I could shower if I was careful. Is that okay?"

"Yes, that's okay," he said. "They know what they're doing in Mexico. I have a colleague who got his degree at Guadalajara. He's a fine physician."

"Can you recommend a place for physical therapy?" Margo asked him.

"Sure. Where do you live?"

"In Hastings."

He named the place in Dobbs Ferry where Jack had gone for rehab after his stroke, and she thanked him. While Tricia got dressed she reflected on the fact that all their doctors were immigrants, and she wondered what would happen to the healthcare system if the government ever stopped the flow of immigration.

That Friday was the last day of school, and since she hadn't yet found time to eat a meal at Anthony's restaurant she took Lindsey, Keira, and Tricia there for dinner that night, having made a reservation for four. Anthony greeted them and led them to a prime table near the front window and gave them each a menu and asked if they would like a pot of tea.

"Yes, thank you," Margo said.

"He doesn't have wine?" Tricia asked her.

"He doesn't have a liquor license, and he doesn't plan to get one." She knew that getting a liquor license was a long, difficult process, and she believed that most people were perfectly happy to drink tea at a Chinese restaurant.

"Has he thought of having people bring their own wine?"

"I think he'd need a license for that."

"Mm, let's see," Lindsey said, getting out her phone. After making an inquiry she said: "Yeah, he'd need a license. So forget about wine."

"If you're still taking antibiotics," Margo told Tricia, "you can't drink alcohol."

"I'm done with the antibiotics," Tricia said. "My last day was yesterday."

"Then we can have wine when we get home."

After perusing the menus they agreed to order shrimp shu mai and pork dumpings as appetizers and chicken with basil, eggplant stuffed with shrimp, and pork chow fun as main courses. Anthony took their orders, but he could have used a waiter because the tables were filled and he was running around like crazy.

They shared the food, eating with forks except for Tricia, who wielded her chopsticks expertly.

"How did you learn to use chopsticks?" Keira asked.

"She had a Chinese boyfriend," Lindsey said.

"He wasn't Chinese, he was Korean," Tricia said.

Margo remembered him, a friendly guy with a degree in chemistry who was working on a project to make soda bottles out of a biodegradable material. "What happened to him?"

"I don't know. I lost track of him."

"Will you teach me how to use chopsticks?" Keira asked.

"Sure." Tricia picked up the package of unused chopsticks next to Keira's plate and tore the paper. She showed Keira how to hold the chopsticks, and then she handed them over to her.

Keira had a little trouble at first, but then she got the hang of it, and she continued eating with the chopsticks, though she struggled to pick up individual grains of rice.

When they had finished the gratis dessert of pineapple chunks Anthony came over and asked them how they liked the food.

"I loved it," Keira told him. "It's the best Chinese food I ever had."

"I agree," Tricia said.

"Yeah, it was the best," Lindsey said.

"It was excellent," Margo said, "but I think you need to hire a waiter. You can't do everything yourself."

"I've come to that conclusion," Anthony said. "I'm going to hire a waiter and a busser."

"Where will you find them?"

"In Flushing, where I found the chef."

"How will they get here?"

"They'll come in a van," he said. "There's a service that brings employees to Chinese restaurants in Westchester."

"If you're going to add employees," Margo said, "we'll have to talk with Greta about it."

"I'll let you know when I've found them."

When she tried to pay the check he wouldn't let her, and she knew he would be offended if she left a tip, so she thanked him for the meal and told him that next time she would pay.

On Monday since Keira didn't have school she spent the morning and early afternoon at the café, where she helped by bringing food to customers, cleaning and setting the tables, and running the dishwasher. She was very good with the customers, who indulged her because of her age, but she even got a compliment from Greta, who asked her to take a sandwich back to the kitchen for more lettuce. As Margo watched her dealing with customers she noticed how much Keira liked helping people, and from this experience she seemed to be discovering a new value of herself as a person. When she wasn't busy she read a book from the library, and when it was time to close the café she helped with the transition to the restaurant, covering the tables with white cloths and setting them with plates, glasses, teacups, and utensils. By the end of the day they established a routine in which Keira would spend Mondays,

Wednesdays, and Fridays at the café and Tuesdays and Thursdays with her friend Lisa, whose mother would take them to the village pool, weather permitting.

After closing the café they went home and hung out in the kitchen and played several games of checkers. When Lindsey came home, looking wiped out, she paused before going upstairs to change her clothes and asked Keira: "How's your job?"

"I like it," Keira said.

"Do you like your boss?" Lindsey joked.

"Oh, she's all right. But I really like the customers. They were so nice to me. And even Mrs. Salvatore was nice to me."

"Where did you get the idea she wouldn't be nice to you?" Margo asked.

"Well, you said she was picky."

"She really is picky. But that's a way of saying she has high standards."

Lindsey went and hugged her daughter, saying: "I love you. And I'm glad you like working at the café."

The next day, after closing the café, she drove Tricia to Dobbs Ferry for her first physical therapy session. On the way, along Route 9, a big white SUV swerved over the center line and forced her onto the shoulder to avoid having a head-on. The driver, oblivious, kept going while Margo got back onto the road, muttering: "You frickin asshole!"

"He was on his phone," Tricia said, "texting."

"They should take away his license permanently."

"And send him to prison. It's unbelievable how many people think they can text while driving a car. Or how many people can't read signs."

"That's why I don't drive now any more than I have to."

They arrived at the rehab center without any further incident, and after filling out some papers Tricia was led by a trim young woman through a door, which closed behind them, and Margo remained in the waiting area. Knowing that the session would take an hour, she had brought a book, but for a long time she didn't open it. Instead, she sat there remembering the times she had come here to see Jack after his stroke. They had sent him here for rehab after a week in the hospital and put him in a double room on the main floor. The stroke had effectively paralyzed him on his right side. When he tried to speak he couldn't make the words come out, and when he tried to do anything he couldn't use his right arm. And it saddened her to see him this way, so quiet and helpless, a man who enjoyed conversing with people and doing things for them. At the time he was only sixty-two, and he had planned to keep working indefinitely. His plumbing and heating business was doing well, and he was still able to lift toilets and boilers without the help of an assistant. Of course he was determined to do things alone. Though he might have let a son help him for the purpose of training a successor, he didn't have a son, and he didn't even joke about his daughters taking over the business.

Over the years he had done so many things for people in the community, but one thing stood out in her memory, maybe because it caused an argument. It happened more than ten years ago during a blizzard when driving conditions were so dangerous that the governor ordered people to stay off the roads. In the early morning the phone rang, and it was a woman whose heating system had stopped working during the night. The outside temperature was in the low twenties, and the temperature of her house had fallen below forty, and she was worried about her pipes freezing, though she should have worried about herself freezing. There was almost three feet of snow on the ground, and the wind was blowing it into drifts. The village plows were out trying to clear the roads, but the snow kept falling.

The woman, in her eighties, was a longtime client. Jack had installed her present boiler, replacing one that had broken down. It was the same kind of boiler they had at their house, so he knew its quirks.

"I hope you're not going out in this storm," Margo told him after he had explained the woman's problem.

"I only have to replace a part," Jack said. "It won't take long."

"But the governor said to stay off the roads."

"He meant people who don't have a reason to go somewhere. I have a reason. If I don't fix her boiler, she'll freeze to death."

"She has a son who lives in Dobbs Ferry. She should get him to help her."

"Her son doesn't know shit about boilers. He doesn't even know how to change a lightbulb."

"But there's a mountain of snow in our driveway."

"I can shovel it," Jack said.

"Yeah. And have a heart attack."

"My heart's fine. And I'll take it slow. I have at least two hours before the temperature in her house goes below freezing."

"But even if you could get your van out of the driveway, how would you get to her house?"

"They're plowing Broadway, and they're also plowing the main streets, so by the time I get my van out, they should have plowed her street."

"What if they haven't plowed her street?"

"Then I'll leave my van and walk to her house. I only have to carry the part and a small wrench."

"Well, isn't there some emergency service she could call?"

"Yeah," he said, smiling. "There is. It's me."

So she helped him shovel out their driveway. The snow was wet and heavy, so they didn't load much onto their shovels, and it took them more than an hour to clear enough away so he could get his van out.

"Why don't I go with you?" she said.

"No," he said, shaking his head. "I want you to be safe at home."

That didn't reassure her, and she made him promise to let her know when he arrived at the woman's house.

But he did better than that. He phoned her when he got to Five Corners, he phoned her when he parked his van in front of the woman's house, and he phoned her about a half hour later when the job was done. Until he returned she worried about him, but as soon as he was safely home it was easy to forgive him for making her worry.

Fourth of July occurred during the second week of Tricia's therapy, falling on a Thursday, which meant that a lot of people would also take Friday off. As far back as Margo could remember the Fourth was a major holiday in her family with her father being a veteran of World War II, and they always had a party at their house, attended by immediate members of the family as well as some remote members. She continued this tradition after her mother died, and she passed it to Shannon after Jack died. So on Thursday she drove Lindsey, Tricia, and Keira to Hartsdale.

Shannon's house was in a neighborhood called Poets Corner because the streets were named after famous poets, including Shakespeare, Tennyson, and Poe. The houses were built in the postwar era, and they were typical suburban homes, some of them partly faced with brick or stone, and all of them with front lawns, garages, and driveways. Shannon's house, though it was now almost seventy-five years old, still felt new to Margo, and it represented a lifestyle that she had never experienced. Unlike the neighborhood where she lived, this neighborhood didn't have sidewalks because it wasn't designed for people, it was designed for cars. If you had to shop for groceries, or go to the drugstore, or go to work, or go to church you needed a car, which you drove wherever you had to go. There were two cars now in Shannon's driveway, one for her and one for Conor, and when their kids were old enough there would probably be a car for them.

They parked on the street in front of Shannon's house and went around to the backyard, where Conor was standing at the grill. He hugged her, being careful not to stick her with his long fork, and then he greeted Lindsey, Tricia, and Keira, who was carrying the potato salad that Margo had made. At that moment Shannon appeared at the back door, greeted them, and asked Keira to bring the potato salad into the kitchen. Conor invited them to help themselves to beer or soda in a cooler on a nearby table.

She was running her hand through the icy water in the cooler, searching for a beer, when Shannon's kids presented themselves. Sean, at eleven, was a gangly boy with dark hair and dark eyes like his father, and Patty, at thirteen, was a pretty girl, with reddish blond hair and blue eyes like her mother. Margo noticed that she was thinner than she had been at Easter, but otherwise she looked the same as usual. Unlike her boisterous brother she was quiet and shy. They talked for a while, and Margo learned that they were going away to tennis camp next week.

She had just cracked open a can of beer when her brother, Patrick, arrived with his wife, Donna. He was eight years younger than Margo, the youngest child in the family, the last child, as if their parents had decided to stop having children when they finally had a son. With three older sisters he should have been spoiled, but he wasn't. He learned about girls from his older sisters, and girls were always attracted to him, maybe because they sensed that he liked them. He followed their father's advice to learn a trade, and he was licensed as an electrician when he was in his mid-twenties. For several years he worked for a large construction company in Yonkers, and then, encouraged by their father, he went out on his own. He waited until his business was established, and then he married Donna, who was from Yonkers. They bought a house in Yonkers near St. Brigid, and they raised two children, a boy and a girl, who both completed bachelor's degrees at St. Catherine College, the boy in business and the girl in nursing. The boy, who was thirty now, worked at a bank in the city and was married to a girl from Long Island. They lived in an apartment in White Plains. The girl, who was twenty-seven now, worked at a hospital in Mr. Kisco and was single. She shared an apartment near the hospital with another nurse.

While Donna went up the back steps and into the kitchen to see if she could help with the food, Patrick cracked open a beer and joined Margo, who by now was sitting in a web chair, away from the grill. He began their conversation by explaining that his son and daughter were absent today because his son was spending the holiday with his wife's family on Long Island and his daughter was on duty at the hospital. And then he asked: "Is Tricia all right?"

"Yeah, she's recovering from an accident."

"I noticed she was limping, so I asked her what happened to her leg. She told me she was with her boyfriend in a bar in Mexico City, and a guy suddenly came in and killed her boyfriend and shot her accidentally."

She remembered that Patrick and Donna had come out the back door, so he must have encountered Tricia in the kitchen. "Well, thank God she was only wounded in her leg."

"Yeah, it could have been worse. Was her boyfriend a drug dealer?"

"That's what we think, but we don't have much information."

"If she was hanging out with a drug dealer," Patrick said after a pause, "the police must have questioned her."

"They must have, but she didn't mention it. I think their first priority was getting her to a hospital."

"I assume she didn't know her boyfriend was a drug dealer."

"She says she didn't, and I believe her."

"Did you ever meet him?"

"I met him once. She brought him to Tierney's."

"And what did you think of him?"

"I didn't trust him. He was so smooth and charming."

"Did you tell her you didn't trust him?"

"Yeah. But of course she didn't listen to me."

Patrick took a long swig of beer and then he said: "Well, I hope she's learned from that experience. The next time she might not be so lucky."

"I think she's learned from it. She's living with me now, and she's getting along with Lindsey."

"That's good. So how's your business?"

"It's doing well. Do you like Chinese food?"

"Donna likes it."

"Then why don't you take her out to dinner at our restaurant."

"You have a Chinese restaurant?"

"Yeah. They doubled my rent," she explained, "and I had to expand so I could pay it. The Chinese restaurant uses the space I wasn't using in the evening, and my partner pays half the rent and utilities."

"Who's your partner?"

"A guy who had the idea of opening a Chinese restaurant there. I mean, not a takeout place but a restaurant where people can sit at tables and enjoy upscale Chinese food."

"Wow," Patrick said, amazed. "Is the food really good?"

"Of course it is. We have a chef from Hong Kong."

"So maybe we'll try it," Patrick said. "Have you heard anything from Colleen lately?"

"Yeah. I talked with her a week ago." Colleen had married a guy who worked at one of the private ship-repair companies that occupied the old Brooklyn Navy Yard, and they had moved to Virginia Beach after he got a job with a company in Norfolk that had contracts with the Navy. The last time she had seen Colleen was at their mother's funeral, and she hadn't seen Colleen's kids in many years. But she talked with Colleen on the phone once or twice a month. She was the one who always made the phone call. "They're enjoying retirement. They bought a boat that they use for fishing."

"Fishing? That sounds relaxing. Mm, do you smell those ribs? Where did Conor learn to grill such amazing ribs?"

"I don't know. I guess he was born with a talent for grilling."

"Well, that's one of the many talents I don't have."

"And I don't have. But I'd much rather cook on a stove."

After the next physical therapy session they drove to Tarrytown, and Tricia went to the post office to get the mail she had put on hold. She also filled out a form to change her address to Hastings. Within a week she received her credit card statement, which included her medical and hospital expenses in Mexico. It was much less than she would have paid if the shooting had occurred in New York, but it was still a lot of money, and she couldn't pay the full balance, so she only made a payment on it.

A few days later Margo received her credit card statement, which included all the expenses of converting her office to a bedroom, buying an air conditioner for the third floor, and buying a television set. Refusing to incur the exorbitant financing charges, she paid the full amount of the balance, which didn't leave enough money in her checking account to reimburse Lindsey for the expenses of her trip to Mexico, but she hoped she would make enough money from her business so that she could do that by the end of the month.

She had scheduled the physical therapy sessions on Tuesdays and Thursdays from two to three in the afternoon, so on those days Anthony had to be at the café an hour earlier to take over from her. Keira spent those days at Lisa's house or at the village pool with Lisa and her mother, so Margo and Tricia had time together after they came home from therapy. With the heat wave over they hung out on the front porch with Tricia stretched out on a lounge chair and Margo in one of the heavy-duty web chairs that Jack had bought on sale from the local hardware store.

One afternoon, while the workers across the street were high on ladders painting the same spot for the umpteenth time, Tricia began a conversation by saying: "You know, I've been thinking about what I'm going to do when I recover."

Margo waited for her to continue.

"And I've decided that at least for a while I don't want to live by myself. I want to live with you. Would that be okay?"

"Of course it would."

"I could help you at the café."

"Well, we don't have a bar," Margo said, "but there're other things you could do."

"I really want to learn to cook. Do you think Chavo would teach me?"

"I think he would. If you helped him in the kitchen you could learn a lot from him."

"I mean, I don't want to spend my life in a kitchen, but I want to know what happens there."

"That would give you something to do in the mornings, but Peter takes over the kitchen in the afternoons and evenings."

"Who's Peter?"

"Our chef from Hong Kong."

"So you don't think I could learn to chop up food with a cleaver?"

Margo laughed as she was supposed to. "If I was Peter, I wouldn't trust you with a cleaver."

"I wouldn't trust myself with a cleaver." Tricia paused. "I wouldn't expect you to pay me for helping at the café, so I'd need to find a job that pays me. And maybe they could use me at one of the bars in this village."

"Maybe they could. Do you like working as a bartender?"

"Yeah, I do. I like being with people. I like making drinks for them, and I like talking with them."

"Then you wouldn't be happy working in a kitchen."

"No, but I'd be happy helping you."

"Well, bartending runs in our family," Margo said. "Your grandfather worked as a bartender at the Hastings House."

"Was there a bar in that building?"

"Yeah. And a restaurant too. It was the place where everyone hung out. I had my first legal drink there."

"Where did you have your first illegal drink?"

"At a dive south of the bridge."

"The drinking age was eighteen then, wasn't it?"

"Yeah. And we were only sixteen."

"Who were you with?"

"My friend Greta."

"You mean Mrs. Salvatore?"

"Yeah. You know, we weren't always in our seventies."

"Did you have a fake ID?"

"Yeah. A driver's license from Bar Harbor Maine."

"Bar Harbor Maine? Why there?"

"I don't know. I guess because Bar Harbor Maine was too far away for them to check it."

"That's really cool," Tricia said approvingly.

"Your grandfather worked from noon until six, so he was home for dinner with his family. And your grandmother worked as a waitress at an Italian restaurant on Main Street. She worked the lunch hour, so they were both home in the evening."

"They had other jobs before then, didn't they?"

"Oh, yeah. He had a good job at the Anaconda plant, and she had a good job in the office of the plant. But they lost their jobs a few years before the plant closed. A lot of people lost their jobs at that time."

"So which job was Grampa happier doing?"

"Bartending," Margo said, based on her memory. "He liked being with people and talking with them."

"Then maybe it's in my genes."

"Yeah, maybe."

They were silent for a while, and then Tricia said: "I know you didn't trust Diego, and you were right. I had a feeling he might be lying about where his money was coming from, but I wanted to believe him. I wanted to have a good time with him. And I thought I was having a good time when that guy came into the bar and—"

Margo waited, imagining the scene.

"He shot Diego in the face and in the chest," Tricia said intensely. "And then he shot me. There was blood everywhere."

"I'm sorry it happened."

"Well, I'm not sorry. All those years I was doing the same thing over and over. Meeting a guy and having a good time with him. Quitting my job and taking a trip with him and dumping him. What happened in that bar woke me up."

"I understand why it woke you up, but I don't understand why you were doing the same thing over and over."

"I didn't understand until I thought about it lying in bed at that hospital." Tricia paused. "There's something I never told you."

Again Margo waited, knowing there were a lot of things Tricia hadn't told her, just as there were a lot things she hadn't told her own mother. She supposed that all children protected their parents this way.

"When I was in college I met a guy from upstate," Tricia said wistfully. "He was living in the dorm, and he was a junior. He played guitar, and he was majoring in music. I heard him at a college event, and while he was singing something he composed I fell in love with him. I mean, he had such a tender voice, and he sang with such feeling. It melted me. And we started seeing each other. He was the first person I made love with—and the last person. Everything since has been just sex."

Margo was touched, and she waited in suspense for Tricia to continue, believing this story would end badly.

"I didn't know it at the time, but all the musicians were smoking weed. I tried it once, but it didn't do anything for me."

"I tried it once, and it didn't do anything for me either."

"So through the fall we were seeing each other, making love when his roommate was in class, and then he went home for Christmas break. He didn't come from a happy family, and while he was home he got into a fight with his parents. He told me about it over the phone, and two days later he took an overdose of something, his parents wouldn't tell me what, and he died alone in the backyard."

"Oh, God. I'm sorry."

"I wanted to believe it was accidental, that he cared about me enough so he wouldn't want to kill himself, but when I talked with his mother on the phone she said she thought it wasn't accidental. I guess she felt he did it to get back at her. But I don't know."

"Did you go to the funeral?"

"I wasn't invited."

Margo sighed. "I wish you'd told me about it then."

"I didn't want to lay that on you."

"So what were you doing all these years?"

"I don't know. I guess I was trying to avoid being hurt again."

"I understand," Margo said, "but sooner or later we always lose the people we love. I lost my parents, I lost my sister, and I lost my husband. And I'll never get over losing them. But I keep them alive in my heart."

"I kept him alive in my heart," Tricia said solemnly, "so there wasn't room for another guy."

"Well, maybe now you can make room."

"Yeah. Maybe I can."

Remembering what Greta had said about post-traumatic stress disorder, she asked: "Are you sleeping well?"

"As well as usual. I sometimes lie awake at night."

"When you lie awake are you thinking about what happened?"

"Yeah. I remember the blood everywhere."

She could imagine. "When you sleep do you have nightmares about it?"

"No, not really. Sometimes I have weird dreams but not about what happened in that bar."

"Do you think about it during the day?"

"Sometimes I do. But if I'm busy doing something I don't think about it as often. So I need to be doing something."

"In that respect you're just like your father."

"Yeah, he always had to be doing something. After his stroke he hated not being able to work."

"And not being able to talk."

"Well, I know I've been affected mentally by what happened in that bar," Tricia said, nodding, "and I've considered having mental therapy. But my leg comes first, and I think that when I can walk better, I'll feel better."

"I think you will." After his stroke Jack put a priority on recovering his speech and the use of his right arm. He wouldn't have considered mental therapy. "So let's wait until you can walk better, and then we'll see how you feel."

"Okay. And thanks for listening."

"You don't have to thank me. I'm your mother. So whatever's on your mind, I'm here to listen."

WHEN TRICIA HAD completed her month of physical therapy she began spending time in the kitchen with Chavo, with whom she got along very well, and she learned how to make soups and sandwiches. She tried to help with the Chinese food, but she wasn't good with the cleaver, and she had trouble communicating with Peter, who only spoke a few words of English.

On a Friday evening Margo took her to Tierney's, and while talking with the bartender they learned that one of the bartenders was leaving, so there would be an open position. It was during the day, from noon to six, and though it wasn't the busiest time it was busy enough for Tricia to earn some money. Tricia arranged to meet with the owner, who it turned out occasionally went to the bar in Tarrytown where Tricia had worked, and he remembered her, so he didn't hesitate to hire her as a bartender.

A week later she started working at Tierney's, and Margo went there on a Thursday after closing the café. She wanted to see her daughter in action behind a bar, and Tricia was so good at the job she reminded Margo of her father, who had also been so good at this job. It took an outgoing personality with attention to people and their needs, not only for drinks but also for conversation. It definitely required people skills.

As she sat at the bar watching Tricia work she thought about how she had met Jack at this bar, though it hadn't been Tierney's then, it had been O'Grady's. As usual she had gone there on Friday after work to meet Greta, who worked for a company in Yonkers. At the time they were single, they were twenty-four, and they were on the lookout for guys they might consider dating. They had both gone through a few boyfriends, whom they had dated for a while but hadn't fallen in love with. Their mothers were getting a little anxious, but they held out, believing they had plenty of time to find the right partner.

Since Margo could walk to O'Grady's from the real estate firm where she worked she always got there first and took her usual seat at the end of the bar, where there were three seats. She occupied the inside seat, next to the wall, and she reserved the middle seat by placing her pocketbook on it. If she hadn't done that, people would assume the seat was available, but this way at least they would ask if it was. Back then the bartender was a big Irish guy who loved to talk about sports, and though he was a Yankees fan he could relate to Mets fans. In fact, he was so personable he could even relate to Red Sox fans.

After a bit of chitchat with him Margo ordered a glass of the house white wine, which at that time was Carlo Rossi Chablis, and she relaxed and listened to the music. They were playing "Too Much Heaven" by the Bee Gees, at the right volume to provide background. To her right, at the long side of the bar, was a man who had worked with her father at Anaconda, and she nodded to him in recognition. She supposed he had been at the Hastings House earlier while her father was tending bar there and he had come here for a change of scene. The man's wife had died a few years ago, and he was living alone in the building next to where Greta lived with her family. He looked lonely, and Margo's heart went out to him.

When Greta arrived she removed Margo's pocketbook from the middle seat and hung it on the hook under the bar, saying: "Wow, this is heavy. What do you have in here?"

"The usual things," Margo said.

"You know," the bartender told them, "those hooks are only good for up to eighty pounds."

"I'm under that limit."

"Oh, I don't know," Greta said. "It's pretty heavy."

"What are you having?" the bartender asked her. "The usual?"

"Yeah. A glass of Chianti."

"So how was work?" Margo asked while the bartender went to get the Chianti.

"It wasn't so bad," Greta told her. "The accountant was sick, so he wasn't at the office bugging me."

"It wasn't so bad at my office. We had a sale, so everyone was happy."

"What kind of sale? A house?"

"Yeah. It sold for a hundred and fifty thousand."

"Really? I can't imagine paying that much money for a house. How can people afford it?"

"They work on Wall Street," the bartender said, setting the glass of wine on the bar in front of Greta. "That's how."

"I don't understand what they do on Wall Street," Margo said.

"They play with other people's money," the bartender said.

"You make it sound like a casino."

"It is a casino."

"How do you know?"

"I worked there for a while."

They sipped their wine and continued talking. Sooner or later they would get to the subject of their families. They didn't have problems with their parents, but they did have problems with their siblings. They were both the oldest child in their family, and they were both expected to set standards for their younger sisters and brothers. To get away from this situation they fantasized about living together in an apartment, but they would need two bedrooms, and since she worked for a real estate firm Margo knew how much rent they would have to pay for a two-bedroom apartment in the River Villages or in Yonkers, and if they lived up county to get an apartment for less they would need cars, which would cost more than the savings in rent. So they were stuck at home with their siblings.

They were on this subject when a guy came in and asked Greta: "Is this seat available?"

"Yeah, sure," Greta said, removing her pocketbook from it.

The guy was wearing work clothes, which didn't reveal much about his body, but Margo could somehow tell he had a rugged build. With his light wavy hair and ruddy skin and mirthful blue eyes he was probably Irish and definitely attractive.

The bartender, who didn't seem to know him, asked what he would like to drink, and he said Guinness. It didn't take them long to get into a hearty conversation, from which Margo overheard that he was a Yankees fan. When the bartender went to wait on other people the guy turned to his left and asked: "How are you young ladies?"

Getting another look at his face, Margo figured that he was at least thirty, so they must have looked young to him.

"We're doing fine," Greta said.

"I could have asked if you come here often," he told them, "but I figured you were too sophisticated for that line."

"Well, we do come here often, and we haven't seen you here before."

"So what am I doing here?" he asked in good humor. "I'm here because I had a job in this village."

"What kind of job?"

"A plumbing job."

"So you're a plumber?"

"That's what I am. What are you?"

"I'm a bookkeeper."

"And you?" he said, looking at her around Greta.

Their eyes met, and something connected between them. She had to catch her breath before saying: "I'm a secretary."

"So you're both gainfully employed," he said with his eyes still on her.

"We're employed," Greta said, "though not gainfully."

"You mean they don't pay you enough?"

"They don't. But the only way we could make more money is to work in the city, and we don't want to do that."

"Why not?"

"We don't want to commute to the city, and we don't want to live there."

"So you're happy living here?"

"Yeah. We both grew up in this village."

"I assume you both live with your families."

"We do. We were talking about them when you came in."

"You were talking about your families? I can't imagine that," he joked. "I mean, what's there to talk about?"

"Everything," Greta said.

After taking a long sip of Guinness he said: "Yeah, families are the most important thing."

Margo liked his saying that, and she could tell he really meant it. He didn't just say it to make a good impression.

"So where does your family live?" Greta asked him.

"They live in Yonkers, near Sacred Heart."

"Do you live with them?"

"No. I have my own apartment."

It sounded like he lived alone, but as if she wanted to make sure, Greta asked: "Do you live alone?"

"Oh, yeah. I don't have a girlfriend living with me."

"Do you have a girlfriend?"

"What's this?" he asked good-naturedly. "Twenty questions?"

"I'm just trying to determine if you're suitable."

"Suitable for what?"

"For my friend," Greta said. "I can't help noticing how you look at her."

At that point Margo turned red, though she would have been even more embarrassed if the guy hadn't also turned red.

"What are you? A matchmaker?" he said, recovering.

"No, I'm just a friend."

"Well, I'm Jack. And you're?"

"Greta. And this is Margo."

"Greta and Margo. I'm pleased to meet you. Do you come here often?"

They all laughed.

"We come here on Fridays after work."

"To thank God the week is over?"

"Yeah. And to relax."

"So let me buy you another round. Your glasses are empty."

"Can I give you a splash?" Tricia asked her.

"What?" she asked as if she was coming out of a dream. "Oh, yeah."

Tricia promptly got the bottle of wine and filled her glass and asked: "What were you thinking about?"

"I was thinking about how I met your father."

"Where did you meet him?"

"I met him here, where I'm sitting now."

"I didn't know that. I knew you met him in a bar, but I didn't know it was here."

"Yeah. This place was called O'Grady's then, but it hasn't changed, except that the customers are different."

"How are they different?"

"Back then they were mostly working-class people, and now they're mostly young professionals."

"But people your age still come here."

"Yeah. The few who are left."

"You know," Tricia told her. "I like this job. And I think I'd like it even more if I had the night shift, but the day shift's fine. I'm not up to doing the night shift yet."

"Does it bother you being on your feet so long?"

"At times, yeah. But when it's not busy I can sit down. There's a chair behind the bar."

"Then you should rest whenever you can."

She made her splash of wine last until the night bartender arrived, and after Tricia made the transition they walked home together. It was still light, and the temperature was comfortable.

When they entered the house they found Lindsey and Keira in the living room watching a movie on Netflix. Since she didn't feel like watching a movie she left them and followed Tricia upstairs. Once she was on the second floor she somehow found the energy to go up to the third floor, where she sat at her desk and checked the figures that Greta had given her that morning. The income from the café was higher than before the heat wave due to a resumption of people eating out and an increase in deliveries, for which they were using a service, and even with the charge for the service they were making a profit on it. The income from the Chinese restaurant was steadily increasing, and it was doing so well that Greta said she should have gotten a percentage of sales instead of only getting half the rent and utilities. But she had no regrets because she knew that Anthony was trying to save money so he could bring his family to America, and as long as she didn't have any more extraordinary expenses, she would be fine.

The next day, since Keira was at the café helping her, she joined Greta at lunchtime to talk about the figures she had seen the night before. They didn't get to that subject right away because Greta wanted to talk about something that was happening in her building. She began by saying: "I think the guy below me is using his apartment for an Airbnb."

"Really?" Margo said, having heard about people using their homes for this purpose.

"Yeah. I've been seeing people come into the building with wheelies who look like they just got off a plane."

"Are you sure they aren't people he knows?"

"I'm sure they aren't. For one thing, he doesn't live there."

"Where does he live?"

"Somewhere in the city. He inherited the apartment from his mother, and he doesn't want to live there, so he rents it to people, short term, and he probably makes a lot more money than he pays for the apartment, which of course is still under rent control."

"But how can he be a tenant if he doesn't live there?"

"He pretends to live there. He has his bills sent to that address, and he comes and gets his mail every week."

"Well, that's not right," Margo said, knowing how hard it was to find an affordable apartment in the village. "A family could live in that apartment."

"Yeah. It has three bedrooms, just like mine. And from what I've seen, he rents it to tourists who want to stay in a cheap place near the city."

"How much do you think he charges?"

"I don't know. But if he charges a hundred fifty a night, that's cheaper than any hotel in the city, and if he rents it twenty nights a month, he's getting three thousand a month. And he could be getting as much as four thousand."

"That's a lot of money."

"I don't mind him taking advantage of the system, but I do mind having people in the building who I don't know. I mean, they could be involved in criminal activities."

"Like drug dealing," Margo said, thinking of Tricia's most recent boyfriend.

"Or human trafficking. One of the girls looked awfully young."

"Do you hear them at night?"

"I don't hear them in their apartment. That building has thick walls. But sometimes I hear them in the hall. Last night the two guys who are staying there came home drunk, and they were yelling at each other. The woman in the apartment across the hall came out and asked them to go to bed. They laughed and told her to go fuck herself."

"You should complain to the owner of the building."

"I guess I should," Greta said, frowning, "but I don't want to rat the guy out."

"Do you know him?"

"Not really. I know him by sight."

"Well, next time he comes to get his mail you should talk with him and tell him you know what he's doing."

"I could threaten to tell the owner of the building. At least that would give him a warning." Greta was silent, reflecting. "Okay. I'll do that, and I'll see what happens."

Believing they had dealt with that subject, Margo said: "I reviewed the numbers you sent me. They look very good."

"Yeah, the restaurant's already making money. You should've gotten a piece of the action."

"I'm happy with the arrangement I made. He's paying half the rent and utilities, and I'm doing better with the café. I'm even making money on the deliveries."

"He should use that service for the restaurant."

"He should, but he has a problem with doing takeout. He thinks it might lower the image of his place."

"I understand, though I don't agree." Greta paused. "Well, his employees all have social security numbers, so they're all legal."

"Except for him."

"He's not on the payroll, so he should be all right for a while. Is anything happening with his process of getting asylum?"

"Not that I know of, but I haven't asked him lately. I don't want to upset him by bringing up the subject."

"I assume he has a lawyer working on it."

"Yeah. He has a lawyer from Flushing who helps Chinese immigrants."

"Well, it should help his case that he came here to escape from persecution by the government of China. I mean, because of our hostile relations with them."

"I hope it does, but I don't know anything about the process of getting asylum. I just know it's complicated."

"I feel bad," Greta said, "that he had to leave his family in Hong Kong."

"I do too. I can't imagine having to leave my family and go to another country."

"I can't either, though families can be a pain in the ass."

"They can. But they can also be a blessing." She got up from the table in response to a signal from Keira, who was at the counter with a customer who didn't look happy.

The next day, because it was Saturday she left Keira at home with Lindsey, and she stayed at the café after closing time to talk with Anthony, who arrived as usual ahead of the van that brought his employees from Flushing. He was in good spirits, and joining her at a table, he said: "I met with my lawyer this morning, and he thinks I have a very good chance of getting asylum."

"That's great," she said. "Did he say how long it'll take?"

"He said it might not take more than a year. He said I'm in a favorable position because I'm a refugee from China."

"So it's political."

"Everything's political."

"Not everything. Your restaurant isn't political."

He smiled. "So far it isn't, but if there was a war between our countries people might not go to Chinese restaurants."

"My mother told me they didn't go to German restaurants during World War II."

"Are there any German restaurants around here?"

"No, but there's one in Yorktown."

"I've never had German food," he said.

"I only had it once. I liked the Wiener schnitzel and the sauerkraut."

"Is sauerkraut like kimchi?"

"I don't know. What's kimchi?"

"Fermented cabbage. It's Korean."

"Oh, yeah. I remember my daughter brought some home. It was very spicy. At the time she had a Korean boyfriend."

"Well, I don't plan to serve kimchi," he said, "but I'm going to add some items to the menu."

"That sounds good."

"We already have regular customers, so we need to give them more items to choose from."

"Where would you get ideas for new items?"

"Peter could get them. He's always talking with other chefs."

"And they share their secrets?"

"They brag about their creations."

They were silent for a while, and then she asked: "How are your wife and children doing?"

"They're doing okay. Of course they want to come here and join me."

"Do they have to wait until your asylum is approved?"

"My lawyer says they should, but a year is a long time. And I want to get them out of Hong Kong while I still can."

"Has the government done anything to them because of you?"

"They haven't yet. But they could," he added grimly.

"Do you have pictures of them?"

"Of course." He took out his phone and scrolled for a while and showed her a picture, saying: "This is my wife."

She saw a woman who looked younger than Tricia. "She's very pretty."

"Yes, she is." He turned the phone and gazed longingly at the picture. Then he scrolled and showed her another picture, saying: "These are my children."

She saw two children with round faces, bright eyes, and neatly cut bangs. "They're adorable. How old are they?"

"The girl is four, and the boy is two."

"It's good that the girl is older," she said.

"I know what you mean. She loves her little brother."

"My parents had four children, three girls and finally a boy. And we all loved our little brother."

"I miss them," he said, returning the phone to his pants pocket. "And until I have them safely here, I'll worry about them. So I want to get them out of Hong Kong as soon as possible."

"I'll pray for that happening."

"I'm always praying for it," he said, touching the middle of his chest. By now she knew that there was a cross at the end of the cord around his neck, and that his whole family was Catholic, including his wife and children, which didn't help their relations with the government.

When she got home she found Lindsey and Keira in the backyard playing badminton. Jack had bought the game for their children, who had used it for a while and eventually abandoned it. For years it had been lying on the third floor, and Lindsey remembered it and found it. They had set up the net, and they were hitting a bedraggled bird sometimes over it, sometimes into it, and sometimes under it.

Margo sat on the back porch and enjoyed watching them. It brought back memories of the times she had played with Colleen and Audrey and Patrick. The best player was Audrey, a natural athlete. Audrey had died of ovarian cancer about ten years ago, and she was buried in Kingston where she raised her family. Her husband, who remarried, lived in Florida while her son lived in Dallas and her daughter lived in Los Angeles, so Margo hadn't seen them in a while. She missed Audrey, and she prayed that her sister was resting in God's eternal love.

Suddenly the back door opened, and Tricia came out, saying: "Mom, I gotta talk with you."

Margo got up and followed Tricia into the kitchen, saying: "What is it?"

"I got a call from the FBI," Tricia said, standing with a hand on the counter as if to brace herself. There was fear in her eyes.

"What do they want?"

"They want to talk with me."

"About what?" she asked, though she could guess.

"About Diego. They think I might have information about him."

"But you don't, do you?"

"No, I don't. I had no idea that he was a drug dealer. So I don't have anything to tell them."

"Well, if they want to talk with you," she told Tricia, "you have to cooperate with them."

"I know. If I don't cooperate they'll suspect me, won't they?"

"Yeah, they will. When would you meet with them?"

"The agent gave me two possible times—next Wednesday or next Thursday, at ten in the morning." Tricia paused. "Could you come with me?"

"I could, but maybe you should have a lawyer with you."

"He said it's only an interview."

"Still, you should have some legal advice. If we go on Thursday, we'll have time to talk with my lawyer."

"You mean the guy with a sailboat?"

"Yeah. He doesn't handle this kind of case, but he knows the law, and I trust him. And he won't charge me an arm and a leg."

"I'll pay for it," Tricia offered. "I've saved some money from my job."

"Don't worry about it. I'll make an appointment with Robert on Tuesday or Wednesday. Where's the office of the FBI?"

"He gave me the address. It's in the city, down where they have the government buildings."

"So we can get there by train and taxi."

Tricia sighed. "I don't know how they connected me with him."

"You stayed at a hotel with him, didn't you?"

"Yeah. And I booked the room in my name. Oh, how could I have been so fucking stupid?"

"You were deceived by a con man. And when you talk with the FBI you should make them understand that you were the innocent victim of that guy."

"But what was he using me for?"

"I don't know. Maybe for cover. He was doing something illegal in this country or the FBI wouldn't be investigating him."

Tricia sighed again. "I just can't believe I fell for him."

"You probably weren't the only one. He was very smooth and very charming." And very sexy, she didn't add.

"I'm sorry I got you involved in this."

"We'll get through it. Since you don't have any information for them, the FBI will let you alone after you talk with them."

"I hope so," Tricia said gloomily.

Margo approached her and hugged her. "I know you didn't do anything wrong, you only fell for a con man. So tell the truth and always remember that I love you."

"I love you too."

EIGHT

MARGO DIDN'T MENTION to anyone that the FBI wanted to talk with Tricia. She didn't want them to worry about it. And she was resolved not to worry about it because she believed that Tricia had been deceived by Diego, and that she was only guilty of bad judgment. Still, as she lay awake that night she worried that something unexpected might happen, and she remembered what happened to her father, which he told her about shortly before he died. Her father had grown up in Northern Ireland during a time when there were conflicts over its identity. Being Catholic, he was conscious of his inferior status in the colony that the British had carved out of the island, but despite his situation he didn't get involved in the movement to expel the British and unite Ireland. But he had a friend who was involved in that movement, and after the British arrested and imprisoned his friend they summoned her father for questioning. He told them he knew nothing about what his friend was doing, which was true, but they didn't believe him. They searched his house, and in his room they found notes about the movement's activities, which they must have planted there. So following the advice of his parents he fled the country before the British could arrest him.

The next day she contacted Robert, who was on his sailboat in the harbor at Stonington, and after telling him what had happened to Tricia in Mexico City she scheduled an appointment to see him on Tuesday. In the meantime she did her best to reassure Tricia that everything would be all right, though she could tell that the call from the FBI had triggered her memory of the shooting, and she was barely holding herself together.

On Tuesday, as they walked down to Robert's office on Spring

Street, Tricia clutched her arm as if she needed support to keep from falling, and Margo pressed her hand firmly.

Robert, looking tan and relaxed, welcomed them into his office where they sat on the sofa while he settled into his armchair. After the introductory conversation he asked Tricia: "When did the FBI call you?"

"Last Saturday afternoon," Tricia said.

"Who did you talk with?"

"An agent. He gave me his name, and I wrote it down." Tricia found a note in her pocketbook and handed it to Robert.

"So he was working on Saturday. I'm impressed. While I was out sailing on Fisher's Island Sound, that FBI agent was working."

"Don't they usually have someone working on Saturday?" Margo asked.

"Oh, yeah. The junior agents."

"So this isn't coming from the top level?"

"It could be, and they could have delegated it to a lower level." Robert paused, and then he asked Tricia: "When did you meet the guy who was killed in Mexico City?"

"In February," Tricia said.

"So you only knew him for about four months."

Tricia nodded.

"Where did you meet him?"

"In the bar where I was working. He came in and took an empty seat at the bar and ordered an expensive tequila."

"Was he alone?"

"Oh, yeah."

"What time was it?"

"It was after eleven."

"How long did he stay?"

"He stayed until we closed at one."

"And then what happened?"

Tricia looked at Margo as if she didn't want her mother to hear what she was going to say. "He came back to my apartment."

Margo wasn't surprised, though she was disappointed that her daughter hadn't waited a little longer to sleep with him.

"How often did you see him after that?"

"About twice a week."

"So you saw him about twenty times before you went to Mexico with him?"

"Yeah, I guess."

"Now, what did he tell you about himself?"

"He told me he was from a rich family who owned a ranch an hour's drive from Mexico City," Tricia said as if the memory was painful. "He told me the ranch had been in his family since the Spanish came to Mexico five hundred years ago."

"Did he seem to have a lot of money?"

"Yeah. That first night he gave me an enormous tip."

"Did he pay in cash?"

"He always paid in cash."

"How did he dress?"

"Like he went to an Ivy League college."

"Mm. And I assume he was good looking."

"Oh, yeah. He was very attractive."

"Then he should have gone into the movies," Robert said drily.

"Yeah, I can imagine him in the movies," Margo said. "He was a good actor."

"Did you ever suspect he wasn't what he said he was?"

"I never did. Until that guy came into the bar and—" Tricia stopped, closing her eyes.

"That must have been a traumatic experience. Do you think about it often?"

Tricia nodded. "More often than I want to."

"Have you had therapy?"

"I've had physical therapy for my leg."

Robert paused to think. "Did the agent give you a reason why they want to talk with you?"

"He said they wanted information about Diego."

"Did he say it was an interview?"

"Yeah. Does that mean they're not charging me with anything?"

"It does for now. It depends on what they get out of the interview. But since you didn't know anything about that guy, they probably won't get much out of it. My advice is to tell the truth, and to make them understand that you were the victim of a con man."

"That's what I think," Margo said.

"Not only that," Robert said, "but make them understand that you're in shock from being wounded by a gunman who killed a person who was sitting right next to you. Okay?"

"Okay," Tricia said passively.

"She wants me to go with her," Margo said. "Will they allow me to attend the interview?"

"They should allow it. I mean, it's only an interview."

Before they left she thanked Robert and wished him good weather for sailing on his long weekend.

On Thursday morning she and Tricia took a train into the city and a taxi from Grand Central downtown to the Jacob K. Javits Federal Building. It was a big block of a building, and they had to go through a rigorous security process to enter it.

The FBI was on the 23rd floor, and as they rode up in the elevator Margo had butterflies in her stomach. She could only imagine what Tricia was feeling.

They went into an office down the hall, and Tricia checked in with a receptionist who seemed to accept her being accompanied by her mother. Their appointment was at ten, and they were there early, so they had to wait for what seemed like a very long time before a young woman in a navy blue suit came out and asked for Patricia Walsh.

They got up and followed the woman into an interview room, where a man who looked younger than Tricia was sitting at a table. He had short dark hair and steely gray eyes, and he was wearing a plain gray suit, a white shirt, and a blue tie. After introducing the man to them as Agent Gibbs the woman sat down next to him and invited them to sit on the other side of a table.

"This is my mother," Tricia told the agent.

"I'm pleased to meet you," he said. "What's your name?"

"Margo Walsh."

"Well, since this is only an interview it's all right for you to be here, but you're not allowed to participate."

"Okay," she said, though she would have liked to.

"Now, please be on notice," he said to Tricia, "that we're going to record this conversation, so think carefully before you answer my questions. And feel free to correct anything."

"Okay," Tricia said.

"The purpose of this interview is to get any information that you might have about Diego Rodriguez, who's the subject of our investigation. You understand?"

"I understand."

The agent paused to consult his notes, and then he asked: "When did you meet Diego Rodriguez?"

"In February of this year."

As the agent continued, asking the same kind of questions that Robert had asked, Margo realized that Robert had not only been getting information for his record but was also preparing Tricia for this interview.

"So he went to your apartment the night you met him?"

"Yeah, he did," Tricia said, looking embarrassed.

"How many times did he go to your apartment after that?"

"About twice a week."

"And you dated him for about three months before you went to Mexico with him?"

"That's right."

"Is it fair to say he went to your apartment about twenty times?"

"Yeah, I think so."

"Did you ever see him with other people?"

"No. He was always alone."

"Did you know where he lived?"

"He said he lived in Bronxville, where his parents owned a second home."

"Did you ever go there?"

"No. He never asked me to go there."

"Well, didn't that make you wonder about him?"

"No. It wasn't the kind of relationship where I expected him to introduce me to his parents."

"Mm." The agent consulted his notes. "So you went to Mexico City with him. Where did you stay?"

"In a nice hotel." She told him its name.

"And what did you do there?"

"He took me around and showed me the sights, and we ate in fancy restaurants."

"Did he meet with any people there?"

"Not that I know of. We were together all the time."

"So you went to that bar where he was killed. Did he know people there?"

"I don't think so. We just went there for a drink after walking around. We were going to have dinner at a restaurant that he said had the best seafood. In fact, we were about to leave when—" Tricia stopped.

"Tell us what happened."

Tricia took a deep breath. "A guy came into the bar and opened fire. He shot Diego, and he shot me."

"Are you sure it was only one guy?"

"I'm sure. I saw him run out of there."

"Did he say anything to Diego?"

"No. He just shot him."

"Did Diego say anything to you after they shot him?"

"No," Tricia said. "He was dead."

"Okay," the agent said after consulting his notes. "Is there anything you'd like to add?"

"Yeah. There is. I didn't know Diego was a drug dealer. I believed he came from a rich family. I expected to see his family's ranch. I didn't expect to see him killed while he was sitting right next to me, to see his face shattered by bullets. Have you ever seen that happen to someone?"

"No, I haven't," the agent admitted.

"Then you don't know what it's like to see it happen over and over, every day and every night." At that point Tricia started crying.

Margo wanted to comfort her, but she realized that it would be helpful for the agent to see how Tricia was affected by the shooting, so she didn't intervene.

The agent seemed moved. He thanked Tricia and told her that if he had any further questions he would contact her.

Outside of the building Tricia asked if she thought the meeting had gone well, and Margo said she thought it had. Her only concern was the agent's focus on the number of times that Diego had gone to Tricia's apartment, but Tricia assured her that nothing had happened there other than what she would have assumed.

When they returned to Hastings they parted, with Tricia going to her job at Tierney's in time to start her shift, and Margo going to the café in time to relieve Anthony from managing the café. After thanking him she joined Greta who was sitting at her usual table.

"So where've you been?" Greta asked her.

"Oh," she sighed. "It's a long story."

"I want to hear it, but before you tell me your long story I'll tell you my short one."

She waited in expectation.

"Well, I told my landlord about the guy below me using his apartment for an Airbnb, and he came there and caught them in the act."

"Who did he catch?"

"A couple from Georgia who were staying in the apartment. He knocked on the door, and a guy opened it. They were having breakfast, the guy and his wife or girlfriend. And they were surprised to learn that the apartment wasn't supposed to be used for an Airbnb. My landlord, being nice, told them they could stay for one more night while they found another place to stay, and then he called his tenant and told him he no longer had a lease."

"He can do that legally?"

"Oh, yeah. Our leases don't allow us to sublet without his permission. So that guy is gone, and now my landlord can find a tenant who'll actually live in that apartment."

"It would be perfect for a young family with children."

"Yeah. That's what we were when my family moved into that building." Greta paused as if remembering. "He can raise the rent by a certain percentage, but it'll still be affordable."

"Well, that's a good short story."

"Yeah. Now, tell me your long one."

She went back to the beginning when Tricia got the call from the FBI, and she told Greta everything, including what happened at the meeting today with the agent.

When she had concluded, Greta said: "That's a good long story."

"Yeah. And I want to believe that's the end of it."

"But you're still worried."

"Yeah. I am. I mean, I don't have any doubts about Tricia. I know she's innocent. But sometimes being innocent isn't enough."

"I understand," Greta said. Then after a silence she asked: "How did the FBI connect Tricia with that guy?"

"They flew to Mexico City together, and they stayed together in a hotel there, so the FBI could have connected them with information they got from the hotel or from the airline."

"Mm, yeah. Or from immigration. They get your home address and phone number."

"Tricia would have given them her cell phone number, and that's the number the FBI used to call her."

Greta nodded. "So the guy was traveling under his real name."

"It's the name he used with Tricia, and it's the name the FBI used, so it must be his real name."

"Then why didn't he have a problem leaving this country?"

"I don't know. I guess he wasn't on the FBI's list yet."

"Yeah. And he must have bribed the immigration officer to get back into his own county."

"That's what the doctor who treated Tricia said."

"Well, he's on the FBI's list now," Greta said, "or they wouldn't be investigating."

"I wonder what he was doing here."

"Maybe he was representing one of the major cartels there."

"Selling drugs for them?"

"Or managing their money."

"How would he have been managing their money?"

"He could have been laundering their money. Or he could have been investing it."

Something occurred to her. "You know, I assumed he was killed by a rival gang, but maybe he was killed by his own gang. I mean, maybe he was stealing money from them."

"Mm, maybe," Greta said. "That could explain why he felt safe going to Mexico. He hadn't done anything to piss off a rival gang, and he thought he'd gotten away with stealing from his own gang."

"I wish she hadn't gotten involved with that guy."

"Yeah, I do too, but it sounds like the FBI won't bother her any more."

"I hope they don't," Margo said. "She told them everything she knew, so they can't get anything more from her."

Before leaving, Greta suggested that they meet at Tierney's around five, and she welcomed the idea, expecting that after what she had gone through that day she would need a drink and company with a friend that evening.

On her way home from work she bought a pizza for Lindsey and Keira so she wouldn't have to make dinner for them. She found them hanging out in the kitchen, with Keira still in her swimsuit after a day at the pool with her friend Lisa. Though the suit looked dry, she advised Keira to get out of it and hang it on the clothes line so it could air out, and she didn't get any pushback.

When Keira had gone upstairs to change, Lindsey marveled at how the girl always did what Margo said, and she told Lindsey it was because Keira understood that her grandmother expected her to do what she said, which she hoped Lindsey would think about.

After changing into something more casual she left the house and walked to Tierney's, reviewing Tricia's conversation with the FBI agent and focusing on his questions about the number of times that Diego went to her apartment. On the surface it looked like he was trying to determine the intensity of their relationship, but he could have had something else in mind, and it must have been about what Diego was doing in this country. Since according to Tricia he always had a lot of money, it could have been about money. And maybe Greta was right about his role being to manage money for his gang.

Upon entering Tierney's she put these thoughts out of her mind. She took a seat at the end of the bar and placed her pocketbook on the seat next to her, as she always did when she and Greta were meeting here.

Tricia, standing behind the bar, looked happy to see her.

"How are you doing?" she asked Tricia.

"I'm doing better," Tricia said. "I'm glad it's over."

"Me too. But I could use a drink"

"Do you want something stronger than wine?"

"Yeah. I think I do. Why don't you mix something for me."

She watched Tricia pour a clear liquor into a mixer, followed by more ingredients, and then vigorously shake it. She poured it into a martini glass, which she set in front of Margo.

"What's this called?"

"I don't have a name for it yet."

"You invented it?"

"Yeah. In honor of you."

She took a sip, and she liked it. "Maybe you could call it Margo's Bliss."

"That's a good name. I'll put it on the menu."

She was halfway through the drink when Greta joined her, and she easily persuaded her friend to try Tricia's concoction.

By six thirty, as the place filled with people, they were on their second round. They talked, and talked, at times reminiscing about the past, at times commenting about the present, and at times speculating about the future. They had known each other for more than sixty years, so they had a lot to talk about.

It was after eight when Greta said she had to go home, and Margo wondered if she should also go home, but she stayed after Greta had left and had another round.

Sitting where she had sat years ago, she remembered the second time she had seen Jack here. The three of them had talked for a while and then, as if Greta sensed that Margo and Jack were developing a relationship, she invented a reason why she had to go home, and she left them.

Margo didn't know much about this guy. The first time she had learned that he was a plumber, his family lived in Yonkers near Sacred Heart, he had his own apartment, and he lived alone. But before she could find out more about him he said: "So where do you live in Hastings?"

"On a dead-end street east of Broadway."

"Can you be more specific?" he asked, smiling.

"Yeah." She gave him her address.

"What does your father do?"

"He's a bartender."

"Really? Where?"

"At Hastings House."

"I don't know it," he said. "Where is it?"

"It's on Warburton, the corner of Spring Street."

"Why don't you go there?"

"I do go there when he's working. He has the day shift."

"Has he always been a bartender?"

"Oh, no. He worked for Anaconda most of his life, but they laid him off a few years before they closed the plant."

"That was sad," he said with feeling. "My father knows guys who worked there. They spent their best working years there, and they ended up with nothing."

"Yeah. They got a raw deal." Since he had mentioned his father she now had an opening to ask: "What does your father do?"

"He's retired now, but he worked for Con Edison."

"Was he a lineman?"

"No such luck. He worked on the gas lines. He was the guy who went down into the hole and worked while the others stood around and talked. One guy was working, and that was my father, while five guys were doing nothing."

"It sounds like you admire your father."

"Yeah, I do. I learned from my father how to work."

"Did you consider working for Con Edison?"

"No. He warned me not to work for a big company. He advised me to learn a trade so I could be independent of big companies."

"How big is the company you're working for now?"

"It's big enough so I want to go off on my own someday."

She knew her father would approve of that. "What does your mother do?"

"She's retired too. She worked for the city of Yonkers, in the building department. So they both have pensions."

"I wish my father had a pension."

"Anaconda screwed their workers," he said. "The owners of that company should rot in hell."

"I agree." After sipping her wine she asked: "Do you have brothers or sisters?"

"Yeah. I have a sister. She married a guy from New Jersey, and she lives there. She's two years older than me."

"Does she have kids?"

"She has a girl who's six, and a boy who's three."

"I don't know much about New Jersey. I went there once with Greta to Long Beach Island. We had a good time."

"New York has better beaches," he said. "Have you ever been to Jones Beach?"

"My father took us there once when we were kids."

"You have brothers and sisters?"

"I have two sisters and one brother."

"Was your brother the last?"

"How did you guess?"

"You mentioned him last. Anyway, if your parents had three girls they would have kept trying until they had a boy."

"That's what they did. And I'm glad I have a younger brother."

"How old is he now?"

"He's sixteen."

"That's a dangerous age for a boy," he told her with a sparkle in his eye.

"It is? How do you know?"

"I know from being that age once."

"Oh. How long ago was that?"

"It was thirteen years ago."

"Which makes you twenty-nine, right?"

"You're good at math."

"I thought you were older."

"How old did you think I was?"

"At least thirty."

"Well, I'll be thirty in September."

"And I'll be twenty-five in November."

"So now we know our ages."

"Yeah." They gazed at each other as if they had reached a milestone in their relationship.

After an uneventful week she almost stopped thinking about the FBI when Tricia got another call from them. It was in the morning, and Tricia was helping at the café. From her expression as she listened on her phone Margo could tell that something was wrong.

When Tricia ended the call she said: "Let's go outside."

Margo followed her. They didn't stop in front of the café, they walked to Spring Street and turned the corner, where there were no people.

"Was that the FBI?" she asked.

"Yeah," Tricia said. "It was Agent Gibbs. He told me they got a warrant to search my apartment, and they found money under the mattress."

"How much money?"

"Almost twenty thousand dollars."

"Shit. Diego must have hidden it there."

"I told the agent I didn't know about it, but he wants to talk with me again. And this time he sounded different."

"How do you mean?"

"Like he thinks I was involved in whatever Diego was doing."

"Then you better have a lawyer with you this time."

"Yeah." Tricia looked at her in desperation. "I swear to God I didn't know about that money."

"I know you didn't," she assured her. "Don't worry. I'll ask Robert to find a lawyer for you."

"Whatever it costs, I'll pay for it."

"I'll call him now. He might be in his office. It's Tuesday." She got out her phone, and she called Robert. His service answered, so she left a message. "Come on. Let's go back to work."

Tricia didn't budge, she just stood there, and Margo took her by the arm and guided her back to the café, where she sat down at an empty table and stared hopelessly into space.

NINE

A HALF HOUR later she got a call from Robert who told her that if they came to his office now he could see them. She roused Tricia, and they walked down Spring Street to Robert's office.

"Did you have good sailing weather last weekend?" she asked him as she sat down on the sofa with Tricia next to her.

"Oh, yeah. It was perfect."

"Well, I hate to bother you again, but Tricia got another call from the FBI. They told her they searched her apartment, and they found money under the mattress."

He raised his eyebrows. "I'm surprised they did that. She's not a suspect, so they shouldn't have searched her apartment without her permission."

"They didn't ask for her permission."

"Well, how much money did they find?"

"Almost twenty thousand dollars."

"Ooh," Robert said. "That doesn't look good."

"I didn't know the money was there," Tricia told him. "If I *had* known, I wouldn't have left it in the apartment."

"What would you have done with it?"

"I don't know. I would have asked Mom what to do with it."

"And I would have told her to turn it over to the police."

"Okay," Robert said. "I think you have a good argument. If you'd been involved in what that guy was doing, you'd have known about the money, and you'd have taken it from the apartment when you moved out. The FBI must understand that, but they probably believe you're not telling them everything you know."

"So how can I convince them that I *am* telling them everything I know?"

"You can get a lawyer who handles this kind of case. In fact, I have the perfect guy if he's available."

"Wouldn't he charge a lot of money?"

"Don't worry about the money," Margo said.

"I strongly recommend hiring him," Robert told them, "or someone like him. You want to get the FBI off your back, don't you?"

"Yeah. I do," Tricia sighed.

"I've recommended him often, so I can get a good rate from him," Robert told them while he combed through his Rolodex. When he had found the number he punched it into his phone. He listened for a response, and then he left a message. "I'll let you know when I hear from him. Did the agent give you a date for your next interview?"

"No. He asked me to get back to him."

"Then you'll have time to prepare your case."

"What could they do to her?" Margo asked, wanting him to say something that would relieve Tricia's anxiety.

"They could keep asking her for information," Robert said, "but only up to a point. If they wanted to go beyond that point they'd have to charge her with something."

"What could they charge her with?"

"Being an accessory to whatever that guy was doing. But I really don't think they'll go that far. I think they're only fishing."

"Okay." She reached over and took her daughter's hand. "We'll wait to hear from you."

It took two days for Robert to arrange a meeting with the lawyer he recommended, and during that time Tricia fell into a state of depression believing that she might be charged as an accessory to whatever Diego was doing, and that she would be tried and convicted and sentenced to prison. Margo kept reminding her that she was innocent, and that the legal system wouldn't convict an innocent person, but she knew that the system *had* convicted innocent people while letting guilty people get away, so she had to fall back on her faith that Tricia would be saved by her innocence.

They met in the morning at Robert's office. The lawyer, whose name was Jay Reiner, was a rangy man in his mid-fifties with curly salt-and-pepper hair and cunning hazel eyes. After asking some preliminary questions he focused on the money that was found in Tricia's apartment, and then he said: "The FBI could have planted that evidence."

"Why would they have done that?" Robert asked.

"They didn't catch Diego Rodriguez, so they want to catch someone."

"You don't really believe that, do you?

"No. But I want you to see how anything's possible." Jay paused. "What I really think is it might not have been Diego who hid that money under the mattress."

"You do? Why?"

"Because a guy like him wouldn't have hidden that kind of money where anyone could easily find it."

"Where would he have hidden it?"

"In one of those banks that launder money."

"But how would you prove it wasn't Diego who hid that money?"

"I don't know," Jay said. "I need to get more information. First, I'd like to talk with the landlord of that apartment."

"I'll give you his phone number," Tricia said. She took out her phone and scrolled to it and gave it to him.

"And then I'd like to talk with that FBI agent."

"Would he talk with you?" Robert asked.

"He would if I'm representing Tricia."

"You're representing Tricia," Margo said.

"I'll give you the agent's number," Tricia said.

"Now, what was it like," Jay asked her, "to have a guy who was sitting right next to you shot dead?"

"It was horrible."

"Was there a lot of blood?"

"Yeah. There was blood everywhere."

"Do you see it happening over and over in your mind?"

"Yeah. I do. I can't get it out of my mind."

Jay nodded as if he understood. "Could you give me a week before your next interview with the agent?"

"I'll ask for a week."

"Okay," Jay said, rising from the chair where he was sitting. "I need to go to work now."

"What about your fee?" Margo asked him.

"I'll take care of it," Robert said.

"No, you won't."

"Yes, I will. So let him go to work now."

When Jay had gone she thanked Robert but protested against his paying the legal fee. He relented only to the point of her giving him a free lunch at her café sometime in the future.

They left Robert's office and walked up to the library terrace, where they could have privacy, and they sat on a bench that overlooked the Hudson River. It was a nice summer day, and the skyscrapers of Manhattan were clearly visible, as they had been on the day of the attack on the Twin Towers. That morning Margo had just arrived for work at the real estate office when she heard about the attack from a colleague, who suggested they go to the library terrace to see what was happening. They arrived there in time to see the second plane crash into a tower, and seeing the cloud of deadly black smoke she felt it was the end of the world.

As they reviewed the meeting with Jay Reiner she was thankful to hear that Tricia was feeling better now that she had him as her advocate. They believed he knew what he was doing, and they felt he had given them new hope with his theory that it might not have been Diego who hid the money under the mattress. They sat there on the bench for a while speculating on who it might have been, and then they walked back to the café where Margo relieved Anthony in the front and Tricia helped Chavo in the kitchen. Tricia left the café at eleven thirty for her job at Tierney's, and Margo left at three with the feeling that her daughter's case was in good hands, so she should stop worrying about it.

When she got home she had a chance to lie down and rest because Keira was with Lisa for the day, and Lindsey was still at work. She changed out of her work clothes and put on a lounge dress and lay down on her side of the bed, facing where Jack had always slept. This bed had been their base for so many years, she couldn't count the number of nights they had slept here together. Going to bed together was the culmination of their day, and when she woke up during the night and found Jack sleeping next to her it gave her a deep feeling of peace, a feeling she rarely if ever had now. Languidly she reached out and laid her hand on the spot where he would be lying if he was alive, and she closed her eyes, remembering him.

After meeting a second time at Tierney's they started dating, usually having drinks at Tierney's and then going somewhere else. They went to dinner, and they went to the movies. And one night as they were saying goodnight at the front door of her house they kissed for the first time. His mouth was so warm, so tender, so loving that she didn't want the kiss to end. But her mother, who always stayed up waiting for her, rattled the doorknob as if to say they had done enough. And from then on they did their serious kissing in his car, parked on River Street.

After dating for several weeks she decided it was time to introduce him to her parents. Her mother welcomed him as a prospect while her father suspended judgment about him even after finding out that he was a plumber, which should have pleased him because he always urged his children to learn a trade. It wasn't until her father found out that Jack had served in Vietnam that he finally accepted him.

Unless someone pressed him as her father had, Jack didn't talk about his military service. Not that he wasn't proud of it, but he felt that the war in Vietnam had been a mistake. And years later, when their country invaded Afghanistan and then Iraq, he raged against the government for sacrificing fine young people to the god of capitalism.

"Mom, are you home?" Lindsey called her from downstairs.

"Yeah, I'm home," she called back. She checked her watch and saw it was five thirty. "I'll be right down."

For dinner they had hot dogs and corn on the cob, and then they hung out on the front porch until it was time for Keira to go to bed. After kissing Keira goodnight Margo remained on the porch and idly looked at the fireflies that were flashing on and off above her lawn and over the street. She knew they were mating, and she was awed by their system of finding and selecting a mate. It probably worked better than the human system of meeting in bars, though that system had worked well for her, for her brother, for one of her sisters, and for one of her daughters. She wondered if the present system of meeting online worked so well.

As she watched the fireflies she remembered how at their parties on the Fourth of July the kids would go onto the street and catch fireflies, which they kept in small jars that had held Cara Mia artichoke hearts. Jack punched holes into the tops of these jars so the captive fireflies would have air, and after the kids went to bed he released them because he knew from experience that they wouldn't survive a night in the jars. In the morning he told the kids that the fireflies had escaped from the jars, and they believed him.

Her musings were interrupted by the return of Lindsey, who brought the bottle of wine they were drinking.

"Would you like a splash?" Lindsey asked her.

"Yeah. Sure," Margo said, sliding her empty glass to a more convenient position on the table.

As she poured the wine Lindsey said: "It won't take Keira long to go to sleep after a whole day at the pool."

"They say swimming is a good exercise, but I don't know. I haven't been swimming since I was her age."

"I haven't either."

"You know, you were a good swimmer."

"I liked swimming, but when I became a teenager there were so many other things to do."

"Yeah. Things with boys."

Lindsey was silent for a while, and then she said: "I've been looking for a job, and I'm finally going to have an interview."

"For what kind of job?"

"It's with a nonprofit institute that treats the mental health problems of teenagers. I'd be on a team that works with patients and also does research. If I got the job, they'd expect me to complete my master's degree, but they'd pay for it."

"Where would you be working?"

"In White Plains. So I'd have a shorter commuting time."

"Would you have to work on weekends?"

"No. I'd have the same hours as I do now. And I'd have a decent salary," Lindsey added.

"It sounds perfect. When's your interview?"

"It's next Friday."

"You'll do well," Margo assured her. "You probably have more experience than anyone else who applied for the job."

"But I haven't done an interview in a long time."

"Just listen, and ask questions," she said, repeating what Shannon told her when she interviewed for jobs after the real estate firm where she had worked for all those years went out of business.

"I feel that if I get this job I can complete my master's degree."

"Of course you can. You always got the best grades."

"I thought Shannon got better grades."

"She got good grades, but yours were better."

"Well, I hope I get this job," Lindsey said. "I really want it."

On the following Tuesday she got a call from Robert who told her that Jay had completed his investigation and wanted to meet the next day. From the tone of Robert's voice she gathered that Jay had gotten the information he needed to support his theory.

They met at ten in the morning, and after some introductory remarks Jay said: "I talked with the landlord, who told me that the previous tenant of the apartment was a woman who lived there for more than thirty years. She worked at the post office in Tarrytown, and she must have saved money because she never spent it. She never went out, and she never entertained. A few months before Tricia moved into that apartment the woman died of a heart attack, and there was no one for the landlord to contact."

"There were no relatives?" Margo asked.

"That's what he said. So he had to arrange her funeral and her burial."

"Okay," Robert said. "I see how that money could have been hers. But how could you prove it wasn't Diego's?"

"I talked with the FBI agent, and I asked him to give me the serial numbers of the bills they found under the mattress. They were one hundred dollar bills," Jay added, "the favorite bill of people who hide money."

"It's the biggest bill we have," Robert said.

"After some discussion he gave me the serial numbers. He evidently didn't guess what I had in mind."

"What did you have in mind?" Margo asked.

"If the serial numbers were close together it would indicate that the money came from the same source, at the same time. But if they were spread out it would indicate that they came from different sources, at different times."

"What did you find?"

"I found that the numbers were spread out over more than thirty years."

"Which would be the case," Robert said, "if it was money that the woman was saving a hundred dollars at a time."

"Exactly. So it couldn't have been money that Diego was laundering. If it had come from a payment for drugs, the numbers would have been closer together."

"What if it came from something else?"

"If it was any kind of payment for what Diego was doing, the numbers would have been closer together. They wouldn't have been spread out over more than thirty years."

"Did you report your finding to the agent?"

"No. I thought it would be more effective if I did that at a meeting with him. So when's our meeting?"

"Tomorrow," Tricia said.

"That's good timing," Jay said.

"I have a question," Margo said. "You said the woman who hid the money under the mattress lived in that apartment for more than thirty years. So why didn't the landlord change the mattress before Tricia moved into the apartment?"

"How do I know?" Jay said with a shrug. He turned to Tricia and asked: "Did you ask the landlord to change the mattress?"

Tricia shook her head. "No. I didn't have a problem with it."

Margo sighed.

The next day Margo went with Tricia and they met Jay at the office of the FBI. The meeting was at ten, and Agent Gibbs kept them waiting as if to show he had power over them.

In the agent's office Jay introduced himself and related what he had found in his investigation and what he had concluded.

"You make a good case," the agent allowed, "but you can't prove that the money didn't belong to Rodriguez."

"No. I can't. But I also can't prove that the money didn't belong to you."

The agent scowled. "What are you implying?"

"I'm not implying anything. I'm only making the point that it's impossible to prove that the money didn't belong to any particular person. But the serial numbers of those bills strongly indicate that the money belonged to that old woman."

"Maybe, but I still have doubts."

"So you have doubts, but they don't give you the right to persecute an innocent young woman with a disability."

"A disability?" the agent said, looking at Tricia.

"Yeah, a disability. She was sitting right next to a guy who was shot dead, and she sees it happening over and over in her mind. Now, what does that sound like to you?"

"It sounds like post-traumatic stress disorder."

"Yeah, that's what it sounds like to me," Jay said. "So stop persecuting her, or I'll sue you for violating the Americans with Disabilities Act."

"You don't need to go that far."

"I'll go as far as I have to go to get you off her back. Okay?"

"Okay," the agent murmured. Looking at Tricia he said: "I have no further reason to question you."

They celebrated their victory by going to a restaurant in Chinatown that Jay knew about. Besides having a good meal Margo discovered a few dishes that she thought might work at Anthony's restaurant.

The next day Lindsey had her interview with the institute in White Plains, and she felt it went well, but she had to wait until Monday to learn that she had gotten the job. She gave notice to her present employer, and she arranged to start her new job in two weeks so she would have some vacation time.

She was at the village pool with Keira and Lisa when she got a phone call from her ex-husband. He wanted to have Keira for a weekend, which he was entitled to under their divorce agreement, but he hadn't attempted to see his daughter for seven years, and Lindsey was annoyed by his disrupting her life at this time.

Margo heard about it that evening while they were sitting on the porch after Keira had gone to bed. It was a quiet night, and the house across the street was dark as usual.

"He didn't want to see Keira for seven years," Lindsey said, "so why does he want to see her now?"

"I don't know. Did he give you a reason?"

"No. He just insisted on his right."

"As I remember, his right to see his daughter is subject to his being free of drugs. Did he tell you he was free of drugs?"

"Yeah. But he always lied about it. How do I know he's not lying now?"

"Doesn't he have to prove it somehow?"

"I'm sure he does," Lindsey said. "But I can't find the agreement. I put it somewhere, I don't remember where."

"If you can't find it, we can ask Robert. He must have a copy of it." Robert had handled the divorce, which happened not long before Jack died. She remembered Jack saying that with Brandon out of his daughter's life he could die in peace.

"I want to see Robert anyway. Before I let Brandon see Keira I want to know exactly what rights he has."

After thinking about it Margo asked: "Does Keira want to see her father?"

"I don't know if she remembers him. She was only five when we split."

"Well, maybe you should ask her."

"Maybe I should."

"My father was so important to me, I can't imagine growing up without him."

"Your father was a good man," Lindsey said, "unlike Brandon. And I don't want Brandon to mess with my daughter."

"She's his daughter too."

"She's only his daughter biologically. Before we split he didn't act like a father to her. He acted like it was her fault he had to marry me."

In fact, Keira was the reason for their marrying. When Lindsey discovered that she was pregnant they weren't engaged, they weren't even thinking about marrying. And they might not have married if Jack hadn't confronted Brandon and threatened to kill him if he didn't marry Lindsey. "Still, you should ask her."

"Okay. I will, but I'm not going to say anything to her until I talk with Robert."

"So I'll make an appointment with him."

Two days later Robert greeted them at his office, saying: "Long time no see. What's happening now?"

"You remember Lindsey," Margo said.

"Yeah, I remember. We met in this office about seven years ago. Come in and sit down."

Margo sat down in what had become her usual place, and Lindsey sat down next to her. "Did you find the agreement?"

"Of course I found it. I don't lose things in this office."

Looking at the mess of papers around her, Margo said: "I don't know how you can find anything."

"I have a system." Turning to Lindsey he said: "Your mother told me you want to know what rights your ex-husband has to see your daughter."

"Yeah. As we remember, his rights are subject to his being free of drugs. Is that correct?"

"That's correct. And he has to provide a certification to that effect."

"How would he do that?"

"It's a standard process used in various situations. For example, a person who applies for a pilot's job would need to provide a certification that he's free of drugs."

"I certainly hope so," Margo said.

"You don't want your pilot to be wrecked on weed?"

"No. I don't. And I don't want my granddaughter to see her father if he's wrecked on weed."

"So if he wants to see our daughter," Lindsey said, "he needs to provide a certification that he's free of drugs?"

"That's correct."

"But if he shows me a certification, how would I know it's not a fake?"

"You could have the police check it."

"Okay. But even if it's not a fake, how would I know he hasn't gone back on drugs since he got the certification?"

"You wouldn't know. You'd just have to trust him."

"Trust him?" Lindsey said as if the idea was preposterous. "There's no way I could ever trust that son of a bitch."

"Then it's a good thing," Robert said gently, "that you're no longer married to him."

"It's not about our marriage, it's about our daughter."

"Let me ask you," Margo said after thinking about it, "does their daughter have any rights under the agreement?"

"She wasn't a party to it."

"Then Keira has no rights?"

"Not under the agreement, but she does have a right to see her father. You can't stop her from seeing him."

"Even if her father's on drugs?"

"Well, if you could prove that he's on drugs, then you could probably get a restraining order to stop him from seeing her."

Lindsey sighed. "Then I don't know what to do."

"Can I make a suggestion?" Robert asked.

"Yeah. What?"

"Talk to your ex-husband, and see if you can find a way to do what's best for your daughter."

"That's easier said than done."

"I know," Robert said. "But who ever said that being married and having children is easy?"

Margo said nothing.

Lindsey arranged for Brandon to pick up Keira at eleven on Saturday morning, and Margo left Chavo in charge of the café and came home so she could be there when Brandon arrived. He rang the manual bell on the front door, and Lindsey answered it, stepping aside only to let him into the hall and then remaining in his way. Margo was standing at the end of the hall where it led into the dining room. From her position it looked like Brandon had gained weight since the last time she saw him, maybe as a result of being off drugs.

"Before you go any further," Lindsey told him firmly, "I need to see your certification."

"Sure," he said, reaching into a pants pocket. He pulled out a paper that had been folded once and then again, into a square. He unfolded it before he handed it to Lindsey. "Here."

Lindsey scrutinized the paper, and then turning around she said: "Mom, will you look at this?"

Margo advanced into the hall, saying: "Hello, Brandon."

"Hello, Mrs. Walsh," he said as if he was a young man dating Lindsey and hoping for her approval.

Being closer to him, Margo noticed that his hair was thinning. She had never known his exact age, and now she guessed he was over forty. She took the paper from Lindsey and examined it. The form was signed by a medical doctor, and it was also signed by Brandon, whose signature had been notarized, so it looked official, but all it meant was that Brandon was off drugs at the time of his visit to the doctor. It didn't mean he was still off drugs, and since

Margo didn't trust him any more than Lindsey did she asked: "Are you still off drugs?"

"Of course," he said with indignation. "I've been off drugs for more than two years."

If that was true, she wondered, then why hadn't he contacted Lindsey before? Had he been occupied with girlfriends and been dumped by the latest, so now he was lonely? She handed the paper back to Lindsey, saying: "It looks all right."

"So you can have Keira until five this evening," Lindsey told him plainly.

"I'm entitled to have her for the weekend."

"Well, let's start with one day and see how it goes."

He frowned as if he thought she was being unfair, but he finally said: "Okay. But next time I want to have her for the weekend."

Ignoring him, Lindsey called to Keira who was upstairs in her room. It took a while for Keira to come down in jeans and a T-shirt. She didn't look happy to see her father.

"I've missed you," Brandon told her.

She didn't reciprocate. She only stopped at the bottom of the stairs and gazed into the space between her mother and her father.

"He'll bring you home by five," Lindsey told her.

"Where're we going?"

"Wherever you want to go," Brandon said.

"What if I want to go to the moon?"

"Well, I don't have a spaceship, but I do have a car."

Remembering a series of infractions that had led to the suspension of his driver's license, Margo was concerned. "I hope you don't plan to take her very far from here."

"Oh, don't worry. I won't take her to the moon."

"Where will you take her?" Lindsey asked.

"I don't know." He asked Keira: "Would you like to go to the movies?"

"Mm, maybe. I haven't been to a movie since before covid."

"Why don't you take her to lunch," Margo suggested, "so you can get caught up with her."

"Okay," he said. "Do you like pizza?"

"Yeah, I do," Keira said, finally showing a little interest.

"So we'll go and have pizza."

"There's a good place in Dobbs Ferry," Lindsey said. "Keira's been there, so she can tell you where it is."

"Where are you living now?" Margo asked him.

"Yonkers," he said. "I'm renting a one-bedroom apartment in Greystone."

"Greystone? How can you afford to live there?" She had heard customers from Greystone complain about how much rent they paid.

"I have a deal with the landlord."

"Are you still working construction?"

"Yeah. I'm working at a project in Sleepy Hollow."

She supposed it was the project where the General Motors plant had been, a vast development that was obstructing the view of the river.

"Well, be sure to bring her back by five," Lindsey told him.

"Don't worry," he said. He reached out to take Keira's hand, but she didn't let him take it. She docilely followed him out the door after kissing her mother goodbye.

Margo and Lindsey went out onto the front porch, where they watched Keira get into Brandon's car. It was the same car that Margo remembered from seven years ago, which indicated that he wasn't spending his money on cars. As he turned it around to leave the street she prayed that Keira would be safe with him.

"What do you think?" Lindsey asked her.

"I don't know," Margo said. "I don't understand why he wants to see Keira after all these years. He could have changed, but he seems the same to me."

"Yeah. He's full of the same bullshit. Like he has a deal on his apartment."

"From what I've heard, a one-bedroom apartment in Greystone rents for at least three thousand a month."

"I bet he really lives in Glenwood. It's less expensive."

"Well, if he lied about that, I wonder what else he lied about."

"I hate to think," Lindsey said quietly. "Oh, how did I ever fall for that piece of shit?"

"It happens," Margo told her.

They went back into the house, and a half hour later Margo went back to the café where she found work to distract her from worrying about what might happen to Keira in the hands of her father.

TEN

MARGO WAS IN the kitchen preparing dinner, and Lindsey was at the counter having a glass of white wine when Brandon brought Keira home. He didn't come into the house and talk with them, he simply dropped Keira off and drove away. So they were a little surprised when she came into the kitchen at only a few minutes after five.

"Did you have a good time?" Lindsey asked her.

"Oh, yeah," Keira said, heading for the tin on the chair to get a cookie.

"What did you do?"

"We had a pizza, and we hung out."

"Where did you hang out?"

"At his place."

"And what did you do there?"

By then Keira had taken a cookie out of the tin and had begun to munch on it. "He taught me how to play this cool game."

"What kind of game?"

"A game I can play on my phone."

"So what's this cool game about?" Lindsey asked with rising suspicion.

"It's about fighting your way through a forest to get home."

"Who are you fighting?"

"Bad guys."

"And what do you do to them?"

"You kill them with your weapon."

"What kind of weapon?"

"I don't know, but you can fire as many bullets as you want, and when they hit a bad guy it blows him to pieces."

153

Margo didn't like the sound of it, but she let Lindsey handle it.

"Could you show me the game?" Lindsey asked.

"Yeah, sure." Keira took her phone out of a pocket and scrolled to where she wanted to go. She handed the phone to her mother and said: "Just click on that arrow."

Lindsey got into the game and played it for a few minutes before saying: "This is bad. It's all about killing people."

"They're not real people."

"Whether or not they're real, it's teaching you the joy of killing people, and that's bad."

"But it's just a game."

"It's not the kind of game you should be playing," Lindsey said, doing something to shut it down.

"I play checkers with Gramma, and you don't have a problem with that. So why do you have a problem with this?"

"When you play checkers with Gramma you're playing with another human being, not with a machine. And you're not trying to kill her, you're only trying to beat her, using your mind, not a weapon."

Keira made a face. "Well, I don't care what you say. I like that game, and I'm going to play it as much as I want."

"With what?" Lindsey told her, holding the phone.

"That's my phone. Give it back to me."

"I'm not going to give it back to you until you promise not to play that game on it."

"I won't promise not to play it. Give my phone back to me."

Lindsey slid the phone into a pocket of her jeans, saying: "I'll keep the phone while you think about it."

Appealing to her grandmother, Keira said: "Please make her give my phone back to me."

"I don't like games that promote violence," Margo told her, "so I don't want you to play that game. Please do what your mother says."

"I hate you both," Keira said, glaring at them. And then she stormed out of the kitchen.

After a silence Lindsey said: "I guess I don't have to worry about him addicting Keira to drugs. I have to worry about him addicting her to video games."

"Yeah, but you have more control over video games."

"Well, I can't keep her phone indefinitely."

"She's a smart girl," Margo said, "so after playing those games for a while she'd get bored with them."

"I hope she would. They're such a waste of time. One good thing they did at that hospital was take away the patients' phones. In fact, some of those patients had mental problems because of social media."

"What were they being treated for?"

"Depression, anxiety, and eating disorders," Lindsey said, "among other things."

"So how were their problems caused by social media?"

"They were made to feel like losers because of how they looked, or how much they weighed, or how they dressed. You know, the things that teenagers care about."

"Thank God we didn't have social media when you and your sisters were growing up."

"You mean it was hard enough raising children without social media?" Lindsey said with a smile.

"It wasn't easy. But raising children never was easy."

"You didn't have to deal with social media, but you did have to deal with alcohol and drugs—and sex."

"Yeah. We did have to deal with those things."

Having finished her wine, Lindsey got up and went to the refrigerator to get the bottle. "Would you like some wine?"

"At this point I would." She was making chicken with rice for dinner using a recipe she had gotten from Chavo. She had all the ingredients ready, but she didn't want to start cooking as long as Keira was holed up in her room. So she could take a break now.

Lindsey set a glass of wine in front her and then returned to her place at the counter with her own glass. "God dammit. He couldn't just have pizza with her and talk with her. He had to mess with her."

"He probably doesn't know how to talk with her."

"He doesn't really want to be with her. He just wants to have what he's entitled to under our agreement. But for the past seven years he didn't ask to see her. So why now?"

"Maybe he got dumped by a girlfriend, and he's feeling lonely."

"Yeah, maybe. But he never wanted Keira in the first place. In fact, he wanted me to have an abortion."

"He did?" Margo was shocked, though not surprised.

"Yeah. He pushed me to a point where I was even considering it. But then I told you I was pregnant, and you told Dad, and Dad threatened to kill him if he didn't marry me."

She now realized that Jack's intervention had done more than spare Lindsey the embarrassment of being an unwed mother, it might have saved Keira's life. "Thank God he did that."

"Well, I didn't feel thankful at the time," Lindsey said bitterly. "In fact, I blamed Dad for making me marry a guy I never loved."

"You never loved him?"

"No, never. I was physically attracted to him, but I never loved him. I always knew he was a bad guy."

"Mm. Is it possible that you were attracted to him because he was a bad guy?"

"It's possible. But the attraction lasted only until I had sex with him. And then it was over."

Margo reflected. "So how do you feel about it now? Are you glad your father made you marry Brandon?"

"Yeah. I am," Lindsey said without hesitation. "If I hadn't married him, I might not have Keira."

"I didn't know that Brandon wanted you to have an abortion. And it's a good thing your father didn't know. If he had, he really would have killed Brandon."

"I remember how emotional Dad was. I hadn't ever seen him like that before. It was like he was protecting me."

"He was," Margo said. But she realized that without knowing it he was also protecting his unborn granddaughter.

Lindsey went upstairs, and after about ten minutes she returned with Keira, who had a contrite look on her face and stood in front of Margo and said: "I'm sorry I said I hated you. I don't hate you."

"I know you don't," Margo said, embracing her.

"I love you."

"I love you too."

So they had a peaceful dinner. They didn't talk about Brandon or about video games, they talked about the party for Lisa's birthday that her mother was going to have next Friday, discussing what kind of present Keira should buy for her friend.

Margo insisted on cleaning up after dinner so that Lindsey and Keira could go and watch television together, and when she was done she joined them until it was Keira's bedtime. Then while they were upstairs she went out to the front porch and sat with a glass of wine.

The fireflies were still actively pursuing mates, and the house across the street was dark as usual. She wished that someone had bought the house with the intention of living in it. She had been friends with the previous owners, who after retiring moved to the Denver area where their daughter and two grandchildren were living. She missed having neighbors across the street, but this feeling was overwhelmed by a memory that had been aroused by her learning that Brandon wanted Lindsey to have an abortion.

She and Jack had been dating for about six months when he took her to his apartment for the first time. She was amazed by how sparsely it was furnished and how inadequately the kitchen was equipped. It looked as if the apartment was only a place to sleep, to have a cold beer, and to watch television, though on that occasion Jack actually produced a bottle of white wine from the refrigerator and poured her a glass.

She felt that by now they were ready to go beyond kissing, and there on the sofa, in the privacy of his apartment, they did go beyond kissing, but then Jack stopped and said: "You're not on the pill, are you?"

"No," she admitted. She had talked with Greta about getting the pill, but she hadn't done anything about it because it was against the teachings of her church.

"Then we shouldn't go all the way," he told her.

"Well, we could use the rhythm method," she said, believing it was what her parents used or else they would have had more children.

"That isn't foolproof. You could still get pregnant. And of course if you did, I'd marry you, but I don't want a shotgun wedding."

"I don't either."

"So we should wait until we're married."

"Okay. We can wait."

He was silent for a while, and then he said: "I have a reason for being so concerned about getting you pregnant."

She waited, hoping it wasn't something he had done.

"I had a younger sister," he told her, staring sadly toward the wall across the room. "Her name was Darcy. She was two years younger than me, and we were very close."

Not having had an older brother, she could only imagine.

"When she was seventeen, still in high school, she fell in love with a football player, and she had sex with him." Jack paused, closing his eyes as if to blot out the memory. "Of course she got pregnant, and she wanted the guy to marry her, but he denied having sex with her. At that point she didn't know what to do, so she told me about it, and I told her to tell our parents. But she was afraid to tell them, I don't know why, because they loved her and they would have helped her raise the baby. But she wouldn't tell them, and before I could tell them she went to have an abortion."

"Oh, my God," she said, knowing how this was going to end.

"She found a doctor in the city, and I don't know where she got the money to pay him, but she had the abortion, and she got sepsis. She died two days later." By then there were tears streaming from his eyes, which he wiped with the back of his hand. "I feel that if I'd told our parents sooner, she'd be alive now, with a child. But at the time I thought it would be better if she told them herself, and I didn't want to betray her by telling them, so I waited, and she died. And I feel it was my fault."

"It wasn't your fault," she told him. "You told her to do the right thing, and she didn't do it."

"Well, anyway," he said after a moment. "I don't want to go through that again, especially with you."

"So we'll wait."

"Okay."

And they did wait, at least until they were engaged two years later, and by then she was safely on the pill.

By the next morning Lindsey had decided to talk with Brandon about the video game that he had exposed Keira to, and she didn't want to wait until he was entitled to see Keira again, so she called him and asked him to come over that afternoon. It was Sunday, and since he wasn't going to the Yankees game he didn't have a good excuse for not coming. And he agreed to come at around two-thirty.

To avoid involving Keira in the conversation Lindsey arranged to have her spend the afternoon at the pool with Lisa, and she dropped her off at Lisa's house after church.

Margo was sitting on the front porch with Lindsey when Brandon arrived precisely on time. Remembering how he had always been late, whatever the occasion, she wondered if he was trying to impress them with his punctuality.

Lindsey invited him to sit down and offered him a beer, which he accepted and which she went to get for him.

"I hear you have a new pastor," Brandon said.

"He's not new," she said. "He's been with us for two years."

"Well, he's new since the pastor who married me and Lindsey."

"Yeah. He retired." Since Brandon was raised as a Catholic and wasn't divorced, he and Lindsey were married in a wedding Mass at St. Matthew, and only the bride and groom and their immediate families knew it was a shotgun wedding.

"I've thought about going back to church."

"Good. Where would you go?"

"St. Brigid, where I was baptized."

She imagined him taking Keira to St. Brigid on the weekends when he was entitled to have her, and she tried to give him the benefit of a doubt.

Lindsey returned with the beer, which she had poured into a stein, and she sat down.

Brandon took a sip of beer, and then said: "You said you wanted to talk with me."

"Yeah. I do," Lindsey said, sitting forward in her chair. "When Keira got home yesterday she showed us the video game you taught her how to play. And I didn't like it."

"What didn't you like about it?"

"I didn't like the purpose of the game, which is to kill as many people as you can with something like an assault weapon."

"They're not real people."

"That doesn't matter. Those games teach kids the joy of killing people."

"Okay," he said. "What kind of game do you want her to play?"

"I want her to play games with people, not machines, and I want her to play games where she can use her mind, not her reflexes."

"She plays checkers with me," Margo told him. "And she really likes it."

"I don't know how to play checkers."

"She could teach you," Lindsey said. "And if that's not challenging enough, you could learn together how to play chess."

"Chess?" he said as if it was a game for nerds. "What else could we play?"

"Almost anything except video games."

"Then what about poker?"

"I don't want her gambling, and anyway you can't play poker with two players."

"You can play seven card stud with two players."

"You can? But that's only a game of luck."

"It's not only luck. It takes some skill."

Based on attempts to play poker with her friends when they were in high school, Margo said: "I think it takes more skill to play checkers."

"And she already knows how to play checkers." Lindsey said. "So why don't you try it."

"Okay. I'll try it," Brandon finally said.

He stayed for a while, and they talked about the construction project at Sleepy Hollow. He was a union carpenter, and he was doing framing. He said he expected to be employed by the project for the next two years.

When he finished his beer he got up to leave, and before he turned to go down the steps he said: "I got it. Checkers."

After he had gone Lindsey said: "Why did he have to appear now when I'm trying to get my life together?"

"I don't know, but maybe it's better now than later."

"You mean when Keira's a teenager?"

"Yeah. When she's more unstable."

"Was I unstable when I was a teenager?"

They both laughed.

"Well, I don't know what the hell he wants, but I'm not going to let him mess with Keira," Lindsey said with determination.

"He's not going to," Margo assured her.

The next day she had to be at the café early to take the usual Monday deliveries. She valued her suppliers, who had enabled her to stay in business during covid, and evidently they valued her because they never failed to supply items that were scarce during that time. It had helped that a lot of restaurants were closed, that she always paid her bills on time, and that she had personal relationships with her suppliers. Today the deliveries included not only staples for the café but also a batch of specialty items for Anthony's restaurant.

When Chavo arrived she could tell from his eyes that something was troubling him, and they arranged to meet that afternoon when she closed the café. She could stay because

Lindsey was at home with Keira, still on vacation before starting her new job.

The breakfast business was better today. The heat was still with them, but people were evidently getting used to it, walking more slowly, doing less, and resting more. And they could enjoy the cool temperature of her café thanks to the mini split she had installed during the summer after covid when she noticed that the days over ninety degrees were becoming more frequent. The mini split had cost her more than three thousand dollars, but now with the almost endless days over ninety degrees she felt it had been a wise investment.

Greta arrived at her usual time and sat at her usual table, and Margo found an opportunity to join her when all the customers had been taken care of.

"Guess what," Greta said. "We have a new tenant in the apartment that the guy was using for an Airbnb."

"The landlord got rid of him?"

"Yeah. And he rented the apartment to a young family. They're from Ecuador, and they have two kids, a girl eight and a boy six. The father works for a small business in Yonkers, and the mother works at St. John's Hospital. They moved here so they can send their kids to Hastings schools."

"That's great. What does the mother do at the hospital?"

"She's a nursing assistant, but she plans to become a nurse."

"That's good," Margo said. "And what kind of business does the father work for?"

"They install and repair heating and cooling systems. They're in the right business with all that's happening."

"Yeah, I was just thinking what a good thing it was to install the mini split in this place."

"My air conditioner wasn't working very well, so I asked him to have a look at it. He found the problem, and he fixed it."

"I'll have to get his name from you in case I have problems with my air conditioners."

After a pause Greta said: "When we were growing up we didn't have air conditioning. We just opened the windows and let in the cool air from the river."

"That's what we did. And eventually we put fans in the windows of our bedrooms. I didn't have an air conditioner in my house until three years ago."

"I didn't either."

"I miss the sounds I used to hear at night."

"Yeah. That's a cost of being able to sleep at night. I mean, besides the electric bill."

"Since the end of May we haven't had more than a few days under ninety, so our electric bills for this summer are going to be humungous."

"We used to get cool air from Canada, but now they have forest fires, so we only get smoke."

"I feel like we're paying for our sin."

"Which sin?" Greta asked as if there were a lot of them.

"The sin of abusing the earth."

"Yeah. The pope said what we're doing to the earth is a sin of injustice against the next generation. Like the kids of that family from Ecuador. They're such nice kids. And they deserve to inherit an earth that isn't going up in flames."

"Then we have to stop polluting it."

"Well, the most immediate thing we could do," Greta said with a wry smile, "is to stop using our air conditioners. So instead of roasting in hell for our sin we'd roast in our bedrooms."

After closing the café she wiped down the tables while Chavo cleaned up the kitchen, and then they sat down at a table. Though he had been working for seven hours in a hot kitchen, he still looked fresh and full of energy, but his eyes were sad.

"What's wrong?" she asked him.

"My mother," he said. "She's dying of cancer."

"Oh, my God. What kind of cancer?"

"Colon cancer."

She knew from conversations with Chavo that after his father had died his mother returned to Mexico to live with her sister in

Puebla, and that a few years ago the sister died, so his mother was alone except for the occasional company of a niece.

"I have to see her before she dies," Chavo said as if there was no question about it. "But if I leave this country they might not let me back in."

"I thought you had a special status."

"I do but my lawyer says it doesn't guarantee that they'll let me back in."

"So what are you going to do?"

"I'm going to Mexico to see my mother before she dies."

"And if they don't let you back in?"

"Lupe and Pablo will have to move to Mexico and live there."

She understood that if they had to do this it would be the end of their parents' dream. "How old were you when you came here?"

"I was five," he said. "And my sister was eight."

She knew that his sister had married a U.S. citizen several years ago, so she didn't have his problem. "You're twenty-six now, right?"

"Right. So I've lived in this country for twenty-one years."

"And what about Lupe?"

"She was four when her parents brought her here, and she's twenty-three now. So she's lived in this country for nineteen years."

"You've both lived here almost all your lives."

He nodded. "Yeah."

"And your lawyer says your status doesn't guarantee that if you leave this country they'll let you back in?"

"That's what he says."

"Is he an immigration lawyer?"

"Yeah, he's the lawyer that everyone uses."

"Well, let me see if my lawyer can recommend someone. I mean, to get a second opinion."

"Would he charge a lot?"

"Don't worry. I'll pay for it. You're my employee," she explained, "and if I lose you I won't have a business."

"Thank you," he said with eyes that were moist with feeling.

"When do you plan to go to Mexico?"

"As soon as possible. I don't want to wait too long."

"I understand."

After he had left she called Robert, who for once answered the phone right away. "It's me again."

"I know," he said. "Which daughter is it now?"

"It's not a daughter, it's my chef."

"Oh, yeah. The Dreamer." When she was starting her business she asked Robert to confirm that she could legally hire Chavo. "What's his problem?"

She explained why he had to go to Mexico, and why he was worried that if he left the country they might not let him back in.

"This isn't my field, but I know a terrific immigration lawyer. I'll call him, and I'll let you know when he can meet with you. Okay?"

"I'm paying for this one."

"Then I'll ask for a discount."

They arranged to meet two days later at three thirty in the afternoon. Chavo took the evening off from his other job, and he walked with her to Robert's office after they closed the café. The immigration lawyer was waiting for them, sitting where Jay Reiner had sat for Tricia's case. He had peaceful blue eyes and short blond hair with tinges of gray. An attractive man, she guessed he was in his early fifties.

After introductions the man, whose name was Todd Danforth, asked Chavo a series of questions and then explained to Margo: "The purpose of my questions was to determine if your employee meets the eligibility requirements of the Deferred Action for Childhood Arrivals program, known as DACA, which protects immigrants whose parents brought them to this country illegally as children from deportation."

"Does he meet the requirements?" she asked.

"He does. But he needs approval to leave the country, or they won't let him back in. Have you applied for advance parole?" he asked Chavo.

"Yes. I applied for emergency advance parole. I went in person to their office in the city."

"How long ago?"

"About five weeks ago."

"You should have had approval by now," Todd said. "Do you have a copy of your application?"

Chavo handed him the manila envelope that he had been carrying.

Todd opened the envelope and took out some papers, which he perused for a long time. He finally said: "This looks in order. Robert, could you make a copy for me?"

"Sure." Robert reached over and took the papers.

"How soon do you need to go to Mexico?"

"As soon as possible," Chavo said.

"Then I'll try to expedite this for you."

"I have a question," Margo said, worried. "If they approve his application, does it guarantee that they'll let him back into the country?"

"There's no guarantee, but it helps to have an advance parole. If he didn't have one they wouldn't let him back in."

"What else can he do to make sure they let him back in?"

"He can return through a friendly port like New York, where they shouldn't give him any problem. Don't return through Texas," Todd told Chavo. "They're not friendly to immigrants."

"Assuming they do let him back in," she said, "will they eventually let him become a U.S. citizen?"

"DACA doesn't provide a path to citizenship. It only protects people like Chavo from being deported. In fact, it's not a law, it's a presidential order, and it could be rescinded at any time. So they live with uncertainty about their future in our country."

"How many immigrants do we have in that situation?"

"At least five hundred thousand."

"Well, there should be a law that enables them to become citizens."

"There's been a proposal for such a law, called the DREAM Act, but it hasn't been passed by Congress, and in our present situation it won't be passed any time soon."

"I don't understand why politicians don't care about people who contribute so much to our country."

"It's not only the politicians, it's also the people who vote against immigration."

"Well, I don't get it. Do they know they're voting against their parents and grandparents?"

"They're voting to make America white again."

"America never was white," Robert said, back from his copying machine. "It was built on the slavery of nonwhite people."

"I'd still rather live here than in Mexico," Chavo said.

"God bless you," Todd said. "You're our future. So make sure you get back into the country."

Lindsey started her new job on Monday, and when she got home that evening she was like a different person. She was energetic, and her body language was positive.

"Well?" Margo asked her.

"I love it," Lindsey said with a glow in her eyes. "I love the work, and I love the people. I should have done this years ago."

"What matters is that you've done it now."

"Yeah. I've registered for two courses at St. Catherine. One's online, and the other's in person, on Thursday night."

"That'll keep you out of trouble."

Lindsey smiled. "Yeah, it will."

When Lindsey had gone upstairs to change her clothes Keira said: "Mom's in a much better mood now."

"Oh, yeah," Margo said. "It's like night and day."

After a long thoughtful pause Keira said: "If she's going back to school, how can she do that and also do her job?"

"A lot of people work and go to school at the same time. And she only has to go to class one night a week."

"But where will she have dinner when she goes to class?"

"She can grab a sandwich at the college cafeteria."

"Could you give her a sandwich from the café?"

"I could, but she'll go to class directly from work, so I'd have to give it to her the day before, and it wouldn't be fresh."

"Mm. Well, I hope they have fresh sandwiches at the college cafeteria."

"I'm sure they do. If they didn't, then the students would complain."

"The students at my school complain about the food," Keira said, "but that doesn't change things."

Margo laughed, delighted by this observation. "Complaining doesn't always change things, but sometimes it does. So when something isn't right you should complain."

"I never heard any of your customers complain. I mean, except for Mrs. Salvatore, but she's just picky."

"If our other customers don't complain, it's because you're helping to give them good service."

"I like helping," Keira said.

"So help me get things ready for dinner," Margo told her. "You can get the plates and the knives and forks, and set them on the counter."

During dinner Lindsey told them more about her new job, and then after they had done the dishes they went out to the front porch, where they sat and watched the fireflies flashing on and off, pursuing mates. At one point a firefly swooped down over them, flashing its light, and Keira tried to catch it, without success.

It took two weeks for Chavo to receive approval of his application, and during that time Tricia worked with him so she could learn what to do in his absence. By the day of his departure she told Margo that she was ready to take over the kitchen.

That day Chavo brought his wife, Lupe, and their baby boy, Pablo, to the café. Lupe was a student in the nursing program at St. Catherine with one year left to complete her degree. She had two siblings, both born in the U.S., who were in high school and lived with her parents. Her father worked for a landscaping business and her mother cleaned houses. While she was attending evening classes her mother took care of Pablo.

Sitting at a table with Pablo in her lap, she talked about her concern that the government wouldn't let Chavo back into the country, but if that happened she was resolved to join him and live in Mexico, though it would separate her from her family and prevent her from completing her degree.

Margo was outraged that these good people were being harassed by a government that should have appreciated them, but in her position she felt powerless to stop this injustice. All she could do was hope and pray.

ELEVEN

TRICIA OPENED THE café on Monday, and she was in the kitchen when Margo arrived. Because of the continuing heat she was planning to make cold soups for lunch, gazpacho and vichyssoise, and she seemed to have everything under control.

Since Tricia would work at the café until three in the afternoon she had asked the manager at Tierney's to move her to evening shifts, which he had done, so she tended bar on Wednesday, Thursday, and Friday evenings. Margo joked to her that being so busy would keep her out of trouble, but she really wasn't worried about her, seeing how Tricia had changed after what happened to her in Mexico.

There were a few glitches during breakfast, but they were easy to fix, and by lunchtime things were going smoothly. Greta came in at her usual time and sat at her usual table and ordered the gazpacho with a chicken salad sandwich.

"How's the gazpacho," Margo asked, noticing an expression of doubt on her friend's face.

"It's good," Greta said, "but it could be better."

"So go and tell the chef."

Greta got up with her bowl of soup and went into the kitchen. When she returned about ten minutes later she sat down again and resumed eating. "It's excellent now."

"What did you tell her?"

"I told her it needed a bit more vinegar and a pinch of cumin."

"Did you taste the vichyssoise?"

"Yeah. And that needed a bit more salt."

"Well, maybe you can be her food consultant while Chavo's away."

"She asked me to," Greta said as if she would enjoy the role. "Do you know how long Chavo will be away?"

"No, I don't know, and he might not come back."

"What? Why?"

"Our government might not let him back into the country."

"Oh, come on. Why would they do that?"

Margo explained his situation.

"So our government allows him to live here and work like an animal, but if he leaves the country to see his mother before she dies they might not let him back into the country? What kind of government would do that?"

"The kind of government we have."

"Well, they should have to work like Chavo does, instead of sitting on their butts in Washington doing nothing and living lives of luxury on our tax dollars."

"I agree. And the same goes for our local governments who are driving seniors out of their homes with property taxes."

After a silence Greta said: "Have you ever thought of living in another country?"

"No. I haven't. And even if I could find a better place to live, I wouldn't leave my family."

"That's how they get us. They know we wouldn't leave our families. Speaking of which, your youngest is off to a good start here."

"Yeah, I was just thinking about how she's changed since what happened to her in Mexico. At least for now I'm not worried about her. The one I'm worried about is Keira."

"Mm. Did she do something to herself?" Greta asked, knowing about the girl's attempt to pierce her nose.

"No, her father did something to her."

"I thought he disappeared."

"He did, but he reappeared, and he's claiming his right to have her one weekend a month under the divorce agreement."

"He was on drugs, wasn't he?"

"Yeah. But he showed us a certification that he's off drugs, and Lindsey had to let him take his daughter for a day."

"What did he do to her?"

"He showed her how to play a video game on her phone, a game where the object is to kill as many people as you can."

Greta nodded. "One of my grandsons was getting addicted to that kind of game, so his parents took away his phone."

"They completely took it away?"

"Yeah. The kid had a fit, but they held their ground. And he's only twelve, so he can't go and buy himself a phone."

"Lindsey took away Keira's phone, but she said she'd give it back if Keira promised not to use it for playing that kind of game."

"But she could find something else to do with it. You know what I think?" Greta paused. "I think those phones are worse than drugs, including fentanyl."

"You mean because so many people are addicted to them?"

"Yeah, I see people with their eyes glued to their phones while crossing a street, or couples on their phones while they're having dinner at a restaurant. Those damn phones are making people lose the ability to relate to each other."

"Well, at least my children don't have that problem."

"No, but your grandchildren will."

"So what do you think Lindsey should do?"

"She should keep the damn phone so Keira can have a normal childhood."

"Is there such a thing as a normal childhood without a phone?"

"I hope so. Or else we're in trouble. Big trouble."

The next day Keira was going to Lisa's house after school, so Margo lingered in the café after closing time, and she was there when Anthony arrived, an hour early, which gave him an opportunity to tell her what was happening in Hong Kong.

"Things are getting worse there," he said, sitting at a table opposite her. "So I want to get my family out of there now."

"Would your parents come too?"

"No. At their age they don't want to move to a new country. And they don't have a problem with the government."

"What about your wife's parents?"

"They don't have a problem with the government either. Their generation is conservative," he added.

"So when will your family come here?"

"As soon as possible. I'm hoping as early as next week. The government wouldn't let them leave if they knew they were leaving, but I have a way around that problem." He paused. "Our travel agent has a relationship with an immigration officer who will clear their departure. We only have to time their flight for when he's on duty."

"But won't that be tricky?"

"Yeah, it will, but our travel agent will coordinate with the immigration officer, and he'll book the flight for the right time."

Knowing that his apartment had only one bedroom, she asked: "Where will you live when your family gets here?"

"I have a place for us. I've rented a three-bedroom apartment in Yonkers. That way the kids can have their own rooms."

"Can you afford that?"

"The restaurant's doing well, and our parents will help us."

"Can they send money out of Hong Kong?"

"They have bank accounts in London. A lot of people set up bank accounts there before China took over."

"When did that happen?"

"When I was three."

"Did a lot of people leave when China took over?"

"Yeah. They mainly went to London. My parents considered leaving, but they believed that China would stick to the principle of one country, two systems, so they stayed in Hong Kong."

"When did things start to get bad?"

"About four years ago. By then I was out of university and working for the newspaper. But things were moving in that direction, we just didn't notice. We were like the frog in a pot of water that's gradually heated until it boils."

"So China didn't want to have two systems?"

"No. They intended all along to have only one system, which of course is their system."

"And now things are getting worse?"

He nodded. "They arrested two more of my colleagues from the paper, and they sentenced them to five years in prison."

"Good Lord," she said. "I hope your plan works."

"I believe it will," he said steadily.

Imagining what would happen if it didn't work, she had one more thing to hope and pray for.

When she got home the only person there was Tricia, who was resting on her bed. She commended Tricia on the great job she had done at the café, and then she went into her room and changed into a lounge dress. Since the window air conditioning unit had been off all day she turned it on, but the room was brutally hot and humid so she left and closed the door behind her and went downstairs.

In the kitchen she turned on the mini split at high fan, so it would cool the dining room and living room. She got herself a glass of wine and went out to the front porch, where she tried sitting until the heat was too much, and she went back into the house, into the living room, which after the porch felt almost comfortable. She noticed that the framed photos on the side table were out of order, which indicated that someone had been looking at them. Maybe Tricia, who hadn't lived at home for a while.

She walked to the table and arranged the photos the way she liked them. One was of her and her siblings when they were in their twenties. One was of her children when they were five, seven, and ten. One was of her father when he was younger than she was now. One was of her mother when she was in her thirties, looking dark and sultry. And one was of Jack and her on the day of their wedding.

Holding the frame, she felt a pang of loss to see how young they looked. They were looking at each other tenderly, with their noses almost touching as if they were about to kiss. The photo was taken along with others at the banquet center on the river where they had their reception. They were married at St. Matthew in a Mass with music from the church's organist and singer. As she walked up the aisle on the arm of her father she was thrilled by the look of adoration from the man who was going to be her husband, waiting for her below the altar.

When they exchanged vows their voices were clear and affirmative. When they walked down the aisle, married, she felt the support of the people attending. When they finished the photo session at the reception they strode out onto the floor and started the party by dancing to "Love You Inside Out." Through the large windows that faced the river she saw sheets of rain rolling over the Palisades and battering the glass. They had planned to have the cocktail hour out on the terrace, but the storm made that impossible, so people adapted, and they had a good time. In fact, her father was having such a good time that he got the manager to extend the reception for another hour.

It was almost dark by the time they left the banquet center and headed for the Saw Mill River Parkway. With the help of guidebooks from the library she had found an inn for their wedding night in Ridgefield, Connecticut, and a hotel for their honeymoon on Martha's Vineyard. She didn't know where she got the idea to go to these places, but Jack liked the idea, and he made all the arrangements, including a reservation on the ferry for his car. It took them only about an hour to get to Ridgefield, where they checked into the inn and climbed the stairs to their room. They were exhausted, so they reserved a table at the restaurant next door at nine o'clock, and then they crashed on the comfortable bed, still in their clothes.

When she woke from her nap at first she didn't know where she was, but then she saw Jack sleeping beside her, and she rolled over and pressed her face against his chest. He lifted an arm and draped it over her. They got themselves together before nine, and after a long luxurious dinner they walked back to the inn and up the stairs and into their room. It was the first night they spent together, and it would have been enough just being together, husband and wife, in the same bed.

The next day it was still raining, and the storm followed them all the way to Falmouth where they planned to take the ferry to Martha's Vineyard. Their reservation was for noon, and they got into a line of cars that looked like they wouldn't all fit on the ferry. They learned from a uniformed guy that the ferry had been delayed by the weather, and it wasn't expected to resume service until at least three that afternoon. So they left the car and found a nearby pub, where they sat at the bar and killed time.

A few hours later they checked with the uniformed guy, who told them that the ferry wouldn't resume service until the next morning, and that they should leave their car where it was so they would keep their place in line. Since they had to spend the night in Falmouth they walked around and found an inn that had closed for the season but was going to reopen to accommodate people waiting for the ferry. Jack paid for a room on the spot, and they got their luggage from the trunk of his car. Their room was cold because the heat had been turned down, but the landlord assured them that it would be comfortable within a few hours, so they went back to the pub and killed more time, and then they found a restaurant for dinner.

It was after nine when they returned to the inn, and their room wasn't much warmer than before. When she turned down the bedspread and felt the sheets they were ice cold, but to prove his love for her Jack got into the bed first and warmed it for her. With a laugh she told him it was the nicest thing that anyone had ever done for her.

They finally got to Martha's Vineyard by early afternoon the next day. The inn was as beautiful as in the photo, and the woman who greeted them in an English accent was very nice. The restaurant at the inn was supposed to be good, so they made a reservation for dinner.

The woman took them up to their room on the second floor, and they unpacked and got settled. Since the weather had cleared they decided to go out for a walk, and they were heading down the hall when they heard the woman say: "Oh, shit!"

She was in a room with the door open, so they stopped and Jack peered in, asking: "Are you all right?"

"I'm fine, but look at this mess."

They went into the room and saw a flood of water that had come from the bathroom. Jack stepped forward and into the bathroom and after only a moment said: "The toilet's clogged, and someone flushed it."

"God damn them. They checked out in a big hurry. They could at least have had the decency to tell me about this."

After a closer inspection Jack said with delicacy: "They must have put something into the toilet that they shouldn't have."

"You mean a bloody tampon."

"Yeah. Something like that."

"Well, I don't know what I'm going to do. Our plumber will be gone until Tuesday."

"Don't worry," Jack said. "I can help you."

"How can you help me? Do you know how to fix toilets?"

"Yeah. I'm a plumber."

"You're a plumber?" the woman said doubtfully. "You don't look like a plumber."

Margo laughed. "What does he look like?"

"He looks like a movie star."

"Thanks, but I'd rather be a plumber," Jack said. "I'll go and get my tools from the car."

When he had left the room the woman said: "Your husband's very nice."

"We just got married. We're on our honeymoon."

"Oh, I'm sorry. He shouldn't have to deal with shit on his honeymoon."

"It's okay. He likes helping people."

A few minutes later Jack returned with a kit of tools and a coiled snake and went into the bathroom.

"I'll get a mop so I can clean up," the woman said. "I should have known those people were dirtbags."

Margo poked her head into the bathroom where Jack was feeding the snake into the toilet. "How's it going?"

"It's going okay. I just have to push whatever it is through the trap."

She watched him work, impressed by his knowledge and experience. She knew he would succeed in unclogging the toilet. And he finally did.

At that moment the woman reappeared with a mop and a pail.

Jack flushed the toilet, and it worked fine.

"I don't know how I can thank you," the woman said. "Well, I do know. I won't charge you for your room."

"Oh, that's more than the cost of a plumber," Jack told her.

"It's not more than the cost of having a room flooded by a blocked toilet. You saved my life."

Her thoughts were interrupted by the phone ringing, and she went into the kitchen to answer it. Most phone calls were from people trying to sell her something, or fishing for information, or dialing the wrong number, but she saw from the caller ID that it was Shannon.

She answered, saying: "Hi, Shannon."

"Hi, Mom. I hope you're keeping cool in this heat."

"I'm doing okay. What's happening with you?"

"I need to talk with you about something," Shannon said. "Will you be home tonight?"

"Sure. We should be done eating by seven."

"So could I come over and see you then?"

"That would be fine." She wondered what it was. The first thing that came into her mind was that Shannon could have been diagnosed with breast cancer. "I hope you don't have a health problem."

"No, I'm fine. It's Patty. I'll tell you when I see you."

She had just hung up when Lindsey and Keira returned from the pool, looking like they had been in the water too long. They went upstairs to change, and Margo went into the kitchen and opened the refrigerator and got out the food that Tricia had brought home from the café. It was chicken salad and potato salad, enough for four of them, so all she had to do was wash lettuce for a green salad. While she washed the leaves that she had torn off from a head of iceberg she wondered what the problem was with Patty, who as far as she knew had always been in good health and had never gotten into trouble. But with all that had been happening lately to people she cared about she prepared herself for the worst.

She was sitting on the front porch with a glass of wine when Shannon arrived, parking her car in a rarely available spot on the street. She got up and greeted Shannon with a hug at the top of the steps. She could feel stress in the tensed muscles of her daughter's back.

"Would you like something to drink?" she asked.

"No, thanks. I need to keep a clear head."

They sat in chairs that faced the street, where the fireflies were active. It was still warmer than usual, but finally almost comfortable.

"Last week," Shannon began, "we sent Sean and Patty to tennis camp. They both like tennis, and they both wanted to go, so we signed them up for two weeks. But this morning the camp sent Patty home."

"They did? Why?"

"She wasn't eating, and they didn't want to take responsibility. I don't blame them. So they sent her home."

"How long has this been going on?" Margo asked, remembering how thin Patty had looked on the Fourth of July.

"Oh, it's been going on for a while. At first I didn't pay much attention because she's always been a picky eater. But then as she was losing weight I began to worry, so I took her to our family doctor, and he thought she might have an eating disorder."

"You mean like anorexia?"

"Yeah. He recommended a therapist, and Patty started seeing her. When Sean asked if he could go to tennis camp she said she wanted to go too, and the therapist said that the daily routine of the camp might be good for her."

"Did something happen at the camp?"

"No. Something happened on her phone. And thanks to a camp counselor we know what caused her problem." Shannon took a phone out of her pocketbook and scrolled to what she was looking for. She handed the phone to Margo, saying: "This is an image I transferred from her phone."

Margo thought she was beyond shocking, but the image hit her like a kick in the gut. It was a photo of Patty completely naked with a fat belly drooped over her exposed vagina. "Good Lord! This was on her phone?"

"Yeah, along with other images like it."

"But how did they get there?"

"They were sent there by 'friends' on social media."

"People she knows?"

"She may or may not know them. But somehow they got a photo of her and they modified it."

"And they're telling her she's fat?"

"That's the usual message."

"But she's not fat, and she never was."

"I know, but for some reason she believes it, and that's why she won't eat. She thinks she has to lose weight."

"Lord have mercy," she said with compassion for the poor girl. "Why would they do such a thing to her?"

"Because they can do it, thanks to these phones, and if they can do it, they do it, damn them."

"So you blame the phones."

"I blame them for making it easier to do this kind of thing. I mean, it's like the issue with guns. Yeah, guns don't kill people, but they make it easier to kill people, so we need to get rid of them, and if we can't stop the goddam phones from being used by social media to bring out the worst in our children, then we need to get rid of them."

"I assume you took away her phone."

"I not only took it away," Shannon said, grinding her teeth, "I took it down to the basement and I put it on Conor's work bench and I smashed the fucking thing with a hammer."

Imagining the satisfaction it must have given Shannon, she said: "Good. Now, what else are you going to do?"

"I'm taking two weeks off from work so I can be with Patty all day and get her to understand what a gift from God she is for us, so she won't believe malicious lies about her. And I'm going to have her see the therapist three times a week for the rest of the summer."

"If you want, you could bring her here this Sunday, and she could hang out with Keira."

"Yeah, that might be good for her." Shannon paused. "I also joined a group that's pursuing a class action lawsuit against the owners of Facebook, Instagram, YouTube, TikTok, and other social media for what they're doing to our children."

"I like that idea. How big is the group?"

"Well, as of now we have more than three hundred thousand parents. And we not only want to make them pay for the damage they're doing, we want to stop them from doing it. I mean, they're doing it for money, and that's evil. Whoever said money is the root of all evil was absolutely right."

"It was St. Paul," she said. "He said the *love* of money was the root of all evil."

"They do love money, and they love the power of being able to exploit our children. I can't imagine anything more evil."

"I can't either."

"So we're going to stop those fuckers," Shannon said with the determination that had made her successful. "We're going to convict them of crimes against humanity and send them to prison where they belong, the greedy assholes."

After Shannon had gone Margo stayed on the porch for a long time reflecting on their conversation. Of course she hoped that Shannon's group would prevail against the social media companies, but more importantly she hoped that with the love of her parents and the help of her therapist Patty would recover from the eating disorder. She remembered how one of her favorite singers had died from such a disorder, and she was still saddened by that tragic loss. So she ended up praying not only for Patty but also for all the young people who were being exploited by social media.

They had a good week both at the café and the restaurant, and on Saturday during the idle time between closing the café and going back there to help Tricia she did some household chores, which included cleaning the downstairs bathroom. Lindsey had taken Keira to the pool, so there was no one around to tell her she shouldn't be doing this kind of work in the heat, and she enjoyed applying herself to the task.

As she scrubbed the toilet she remembered how Jack installed this bathroom before they moved into the house. At the time she was seven months pregnant with Lindsey, Shannon was two, and they were living in Jack's apartment. Though they were happy there, the apartment had only one bedroom, and it was already crowded with the three of them, so they needed an apartment with at least two bedrooms. They had been looking for such an apartment in Yonkers since she learned she was pregnant, but they hadn't found anything in a decent neighborhood that they could afford, and the only apartments they could afford were at least a half hour's drive away in the north of the county. Jack was willing to live up there, even with a long commute to his job, but Margo's parents didn't like the idea of their living so far away, especially with another grandchild expected within the next two months. So they invited her and Jack to live with them.

Since he had been living on his own for so long Jack strongly resisted the idea of living with her parents, and their conversations became heated. She remembered Jack saying: "I'm your husband. I'm supposed to support you and our kids."

"You *are* supporting us," she said. She had stopped working a month ago, and she didn't plan to go back to work until her baby was at least six months old. But she wouldn't be able to go back to work if they lived far away from her mother.

"I want to pay them rent," Jack said, "but your father doesn't want us to pay it."

"He wants us to save money so we can buy a house."

"But we can't buy a house in this area."

"Not now, but maybe someday we can," she said hopefully. "When you have your own business."

"That's in the future," Jack said. "In the meantime we gotta live somewhere, and I wouldn't mind having a longer commute to my job."

"But if we don't live in this area, my mother won't be able to help with our kids, and then I won't be able to work, so please tell my father you'll pay him rent."

"I already told him that."

"Tell him again. He can be stubborn, just like you."

"You think I'm stubborn?" he asked, affronted.

"Usually you're not," she said, "but at times you are. And you're being stubborn now."

"Well, he's being more stubborn. I'm willing to compromise."

"So what should we propose to him?"

Jack reflected. "How about this? I'll pay him below the market rent, and I'll make up the difference in services."

"What kind of services?"

"Plumbing services. Their house needs a gas boiler instead of that dirty oil burner. And it needs another bathroom. If six people are going to live there, one bathroom won't be enough."

It had been enough for six people while Margo was growing up in that house, but she understood that times had changed. "So make a proposal to him."

"Okay. I will."

Her father accepted Jack's proposal, and by the time there were eight people including five women living in the house it proved to be a good idea to add a bathroom.

Margo was at the café handling takeouts on Monday morning when Anthony arrived much earlier than usual, and she could tell from his face that something had gone wrong. Before he could say anything in front of the customers she took his arm and led him outside, where they stood on the street.

"What happened?" she asked him, though she could guess.

"They changed the immigration officer," he said with glistening eyes. "And they stopped my wife and kids at the airport."

"Oh, God. What did they do to them?"

"They arrested my wife, and they're holding her hostage. They're saying that if I don't go back to Hong Kong, they'll send her to prison."

"How did you learn this?"

"My father called me," he said. "They called him and told him they were holding my wife."

She put a hand on his shoulder, saying: "I'm so sorry."

"I have no choice, but I don't want to abandon the restaurant."

"Don't worry. We can manage."

He gazed at her with gratitude. "You've been such a good partner."

"So have you." She felt he could have been her son, the son that Jack had always wanted. And she hugged him, saying: "I'll pray for you."

Shaking with sobs, he hugged her back.

TWELVE

ANTHONY SCHEDULED HIS flight to Hong Kong so he would have time to settle his things and help Margo deal with the restaurant. Tricia believed she could manage the restaurant and work in the kitchen for breakfast and lunch until Chavo returned, though they were conscious of the possibility that Chavo might not be able to get back into the country. They decided not to plan for that but to deal with it when and if it happened.

The main problem in managing the restaurant was the chef's lack of English, which Anthony had overcome by speaking with him in Chinese. Since neither Margo nor Tricia had any knowledge whatsoever of that language they fell back on the menu, which in traditional Chinese restaurant style provided numbers for all the items as well as the Chinese characters for them below their names in English. Tricia could take the orders in English, write down the numbers, and give the numbers to Peter, who would then know what to cook. According to Anthony the original purpose of the numbers was to enable Chinese waiters and chefs who spoke different regional languages to communicate, so the system was already in place to solve the problem. Their Chinese waiter didn't have that problem because he had learned English from dealing with customers in previous jobs.

Anthony was there for the first night that Tricia managed the restaurant. He persuaded the chef and the waiter to accept her, he introduced her to regular customers, including a Chinese couple from Ardsley, and he prepared for a smooth transition.

His flight departed shortly after one o'clock. Since he had to be at the airport three hours before departure they picked him up in front of his building at nine in the morning with Tricia driving and Margo in the passenger seat. She had opened the café at the usual

185

time and then left Greta in charge with Keira helping until they returned from the airport.

After moving at a crawl up the departure ramp they finally reached a point where they could drop Anthony off. Ignoring the uniformed man who yelled at her, Margo got out of the car while Anthony took his suitcase out of the trunk, and she gave him a long, last hug.

"I hope everything goes as well as possible," she told him.

"I do too," he said with a wan smile.

"Be sure to let me know what happens."

"I will. Or if I can't, my wife will."

She kissed him goodbye, and she got back into the car, crying, disheartened by the thought of what would happen to Anthony and the feeling that she would never see him again.

As they drove away Tricia said: "I don't understand why he has to go back to Hong Kong."

"The government of China," she explained, "is holding his wife hostage, and if he doesn't go back, they'll send her to prison."

"Why would they do that?"

"To make him go back to Hong Kong."

"But why?"

"Because he wrote columns for a newspaper that criticized the government for what they were doing to the people of Hong Kong."

"What were they doing?"

"They were taking away their human rights."

"So what will they do to him?"

"They'll send him to prison."

"For how long?"

"Probably for five years."

"Well, how old is he?"

"He's almost twenty-nine."

Maneuvering out of the departure area, Tricia was silent for a while, and then she said: "If he goes to prison for five years, he'll be the same age as I am now when he gets out."

She understood that Tricia was trying to make her feel better, and she appreciated it, but she still felt sad that he was going to prison. And remembering the pictures he showed her, she said: "It's going to be hard for his wife and children."

"Will they be allowed to see him?"

"I hope so, but I don't know."

Tricia slowed at the flash of brake lights of the car in front of them. "It makes me realize that with all the things that are wrong with this country, it's still better than some other countries."

Of course she knew that compared with Anthony's situation, or Chavo's situation, or billions of other people's situations her challenges were trivial. And it made her give thanks for her own situation.

Over the next two weeks they developed a schedule for managing the café and the restaurant. From eight until three Margo worked in the front of the café while Tricia worked in the kitchen, and then they went home. Tricia rested for a while before returning to manage the restaurant, and around eight Margo joined her and helped her until closing time. It was a grueling schedule, but they believed they could handle the work until Chavo returned, though Margo hadn't heard from him, and she worried about him.

In the meantime Shannon arranged to bring Patty after church the next Sunday so she could go to the pool with Keira. Though they were almost the same age, the girls lived in different towns and went to different schools, so they didn't see each other often, only at family occasions.

Margo had doubts about the wisdom of taking Patty to the pool, where she would wear a swimsuit and have her body assessed by people she didn't know, but Shannon argued that the girl was actually afraid of being seen in a swimsuit by people she did know, and that being with her cousin might give her support.

On Sunday she was joined at Mass by Lindsey, Keira, and Tricia, with the four of them occupying half of the pew. While kneeling after communion she gave thanks for the daughters and the granddaughter who were there, and she prayed for those who weren't there, including her parents, her husband, her younger sister, and last but not least Chavo and Anthony. She prayed that her government would let Chavo back into the country and that the government of China would be lenient with Anthony.

Shannon arrived with Patty after lunch, and the girls scampered upstairs to change into their swimsuits. It could have been Margo's imagination, or her desire to see improvement in Patty's condition, but she thought Patty had gained some weight since the Fourth of July, and when the girls came hopping downstairs in their swimsuits, looking so joyful, she began to feel that taking them to the pool wasn't such a bad idea.

Margo had invited Lindsey to join them, but Lindsey had a previous engagement with her best friend from high school who lived in Nashville and was visiting for the first time in many years. Before driving off to meet her friend at the hotel where she was staying Lindsey gave Keira a hug and told her to have a good time.

The pool wasn't crowded because a lot of people were away, and there were two lounge chairs available in a good spot for Margo and Shannon to watch the girls. There were other kids, mostly younger, and there weren't any boys who looked like potential troublemakers.

Keira and Patty approached the pool with caution and sat down at the edge with their legs in the water and then gradually slipped into the pool. They were both good swimmers, and they made their way together around the pool like otters.

"This is better than going to the pool in our town," Shannon said. "No one here has seen those images."

"Have the kids at her school seen them?"

"Yeah. It's a good school, but it has a few rotten apples."

"Do you know who they are?"

"No, but she knows who they are."

"And she won't tell you?"

"She's afraid I'd complain to their parents. And I would," Shannon added.

"It looks like she's gained some weight."

"She has. She's eating better. I think the therapist is helping her."

"So she has one more year at that school?"

"Yeah. And next year she's going to high school at Maria Regina, where there are no boys. Thank God."

"You think boys are the problem?"

"Oh, yeah," Shannon said. "They're always the problem. Or almost always. Sean's a good boy, God bless him."

"Your father wanted to have a boy."

"Did you want to have one?"

"I did because he wanted one. But I don't wish I had one. I feel blessed that I have you three girls."

"Even with all the stress we've caused you?"

"The stress didn't come from what you did," Margo said after thinking about it. "The stress came from what happened to you."

"So you don't blame us."

"No. I blame the people who caused what happened to you, like whoever posted those images of Patty."

"You know, she's surviving without a phone."

"We didn't have phones, and we survived."

"You survived without a lot of things that we have," Shannon said. "So we could survive without those things."

They watched in silence for a while as Keira and Patty hung out in a corner of the pool, talking and giggling. And she resolved to have the two cousins see each other more often.

That evening, while Lindsey was upstairs putting Keira to bed, Margo was sitting on the front porch with Tricia, talking about the restaurant. The fireflies were flashing on and off, and the house across the street was dark as usual. From a distance came the rumbling of a train.

"You know," Tricia said, with her feet propped up on another chair, "I have three ideas on how we can improve our restaurant business."

"Okay," she said, interested. "Tell me about them."

"Well, I think we should have daily specials. We have regular customers who might want to try something new."

"Have you talked with Peter about it?"

"Yeah. We're finding ways to communicate, and yesterday he asked me to try something he made with scallops. It was really good, and it gave me the idea. I mean, he's been cooking the same dishes for many years, and it could make his job more interesting if we gave him a chance to be creative."

"It sounds like a good idea. How many specials would you have?"

"I don't know. We could start with three."

"Okay. What's your second idea?"

Tricia paused to take a sip of wine. "I've noticed that a lot of people go out to dinner on Sunday, and all the other restaurants in the village are open on Sunday. So why aren't we?"

"The café was never open on Sunday, and when we started the restaurant we kept the same schedule."

"Didn't Anthony want to be open on Sunday?"

"He never mentioned it. He might have had religious reasons."

"He might have," Tricia said. "Chavo told me that Anthony was a serious Catholic."

"So maybe he didn't think it was right to be open on Sundays."

"Yeah, maybe."

"Anyway, the café isn't open on Sunday morning because I'm in church, along with many of my customers. But there's no reason why the restaurant couldn't be open on Sunday evening. Would you be closed on Monday?"

"Yeah. I'd want to give the employees a day off."

"Then I don't have a problem. What's your third idea?"

"Some customers have told me they'd like to have wine with their food, and one asked me if he could bring his own bottle to the restaurant, with a corkage fee. But even for that you need a liquor license. I know it's hard to get a liquor license, and it costs a lot of money, but if we could serve alcoholic drinks we could double what we're making on food."

"I never considered getting a liquor license," she said. "It wouldn't make sense for the café. But it could make sense for the restaurant. Why don't we talk with Robert about it."

"Okay. I know it would take a long time to get a license, but we could at least start the process."

At that moment Lindsey came out with a glass of wine and sat down with them, asking: "What are you guys up to?"

"Oh, we were just talking about the restaurant," Margo said. "Did Keira go to sleep?"

"Yeah. She read for a while, one of the books you got her at the library, and then she was out like a light. I guess I should try reading when I have trouble going to sleep."

"It used to work for me, but it hasn't worked lately."

"How did things go with Keira and Patty?"

"They had a good time," Margo said. "We should get them together more often."

"I wish they lived closer."

"We had cousins living in the same village," Tricia said. "But we didn't see them very often."

She was referring to Patrick's children.

"They were a lot younger than we were," Lindsey said. "But Keira and Patty are close in age."

"Yeah, that makes a difference."

"Patty's going to high school next year, isn't she?"

"She's going to Maria Regina," Margo said.

"I wish I'd gone there," Lindsey said. "It would have prepared me better for college."

"Oh, I wouldn't have liked it there," Tricia said. "I would have missed being with boys."

"Well, I wouldn't have missed being with boys. They were a distraction. And they were always demanding attention."

"Have you thought about sending Keira to Maria Regina?"

"Yeah, I have. But I don't think I can afford it."

"We can afford it," Margo said confidently. "And that way Keira can get together with her cousin more often."

The next morning, right after she opened the café, she got a phone call from a woman she didn't recognize at first. It was Anthony's wife, Lin, who had called to tell her the government had sentenced him to five years in prison. But she said he was in good spirits, and he wanted Margo to know how grateful he was for her giving him a chance to start a business with which he could fulfill his dream of bringing his family to America.

"Are you allowed to see him?" she asked.

"Yes," Lin said, "but not as often as I would like to."

"How are your children?"

"They're okay, but they hadn't seen their father for almost five months, then suddenly he was taken away."

"I'm so sorry. Where are you living?"

"I'm living with my parents, so at least our children have their grandparents."

They talked for several minutes longer, and then ending the conversation she told Lin she would pray for Anthony.

For the rest of the morning she tried to lose herself in the tasks of managing the café but she couldn't stop thinking about Anthony and how he would spend the next five years of his life in a prison cell, and how his children wouldn't have a father for the next five years.

Around noon Greta came in for lunch, and as soon as Margo had a chance she joined Greta and told her what the government of China had done to Anthony, and Greta deeply lamented it. Then, after a long glum silence, Greta said: "At least he left a legacy."

"You mean the restaurant."

"It's doing well. In fact, according to my projections the profits would have been enough to support his family."

"What about the profits before he left?"

"I can give you the numbers. I have them at home."

"He should have those profits. He didn't have a bank account, so he was going to put the profits into his father's bank account."

"You could do that. Do you know the bank and the account number?"

"He left that information with me, so I'll put the profits he earned until he left into his father's bank account. And I think I should give him a share of the future profits. What do you think?"

"I think you should," Greta said. "He started the business."

She thought about it, and then she said: "Tricia should have a share of the profits. She has some good ideas on how to improve the business."

"What about you?"

"I didn't go into that business to make a profit. I only did it to pay half of the doubled rent."

"Okay. Then you could pay Tricia a salary and have her share the future profits fifty-fifty with Anthony."

"That sounds fair. Could you do the numbers and see what it looks like?"

"Sure. And is it okay if I tip Keira?"

"Yeah, it's okay," she said, liking the idea. "Keira deserves it."

As she was walking home that afternoon, going north on Warburton, a young man hailed her from a blue van that pulled over toward the curb beside her. It was Jack's van, and the young man was Ricky, who had worked as Jack's apprentice for several years and had passed the exam for a master plumber license a few months before Jack died.

"Hey, Mrs. Walsh," he said brightly. "It's good to see you. How are you doing?"

"I'm doing fine," she said, approaching the van. "How are you doing?"

"My business is doing well. And guess what?"

She waited expectantly.

"I'm getting married this October."

"Really? That's wonderful." She assumed he was marrying the nice young woman that he had introduced her to last winter. "Congratulations!"

"Your family will get an invitation."

"Where's the wedding?"

"At her church, St. Brigid."

"That's where my brother Patrick was married."

Since the van was partly blocking the street a car honked.

"*Cálmate*," Ricky muttered at the honker. "Well, I better go. We'll talk later."

"Take care," she told him.

"You too."

She watched him drive away, and as she continued walking she remembered how Jack had taken on Ricky as an apprentice. After weeks of therapy he could talk pretty well but he had trouble controlling the movement of his right arm and his right leg. He could walk with a cane, and he could do things around the house, but he couldn't do plumbing. And being deprived of work he was going crazy.

"I feel so useless," he kept saying.

"You're not useless. You can do almost everything."

"I can't do my work."

"Well, there's more to life than work."

"There is? What?"

"There's our family."

"Yeah, I'm sorry," he said. "I didn't mean that our family isn't important, but I need to work. I mean, I'm just not cut out to be a man of leisure."

"So maybe if you got an assistant you could do the work."

"An assistant? I've never needed an assistant."

"I know. But you need one now."

Jack frowned. "If I hired some kid, he wouldn't know how to do anything."

"He would if you teach him."

"How could I teach him?"

"You could share your knowledge and experience with him. You could tell him step by step what to do, and you could make sure he does it right."

After a long, heavy silence Jack asked: "Well, how could I find someone to hire?"

"You could call Saunders and see if they know anyone who might be interested." Saunders was a reputable trades and technical high school in Yonkers. "Remember the guy who repaired the transmission of your van?"

"Oh, yeah. What was his name?"

"I don't remember, but you said he did a great job."

"He did. I mean, I haven't had any trouble with it."

"Well, he was a graduate of Saunders," she reminded him. "So call Saunders."

He did, and within a week he had three candidates, whom he interviewed on the front porch. After some deliberation he selected Ricky, the middle son of a family that had immigrated from the Dominican Republic. Ricky was an attractive young man who had just turned twenty. He was working in a shop on Saw Mill River Road at a job that led nowhere, and he was eager to learn the plumbing trade. Jack immediately liked him, and he checked the references that Ricky had given, including a teacher who had nothing but good things to say about him. For Jack the most important thing was that Ricky had been a very good student.

Ricky gave notice to his employer and started working for Jack two weeks later. Jack hadn't been working for several months, but over the years he had developed a list of clients, and after Margo let them know he was working again they started calling with their problems. In the morning Ricky took a bus from Yonkers to their house, where Jack was waiting for him, and off they would go in the van with Ricky driving.

Ricky was a steady, methodical learner, and Jack was satisfied with his progress, but the breakthrough came when Ricky solved a problem all by himself. From that point on they bonded like father and son.

Since the next weekend was Brandon's time to spend with Keira he picked her up at eleven on Saturday as he had a month ago. Legally, he had a right to have her for the whole weekend, but he had told Lindsey he would only take Keira for the day, so she didn't pack to spend the night.

When Margo came home with Tricia after closing the café they found Lindsey sitting on the front porch, reading some printed material about the courses she would take that fall to continue in the master's program. While Tricia went upstairs to rest for an hour Margo sat down with Lindsey, and they talked about how they would schedule things around her need to attend classes and her need to do homework.

Then, changing the subject, Lindsey said: "You know, it's like he didn't want her for the whole weekend."

"Maybe he's just taking things slowly."

"Maybe, but it's not like him."

"Well, let's wait and see how things went today."

They didn't have to wait long because Brandon brought Keira home shortly after four, and she went directly into the house, pausing only to greet them.

"Could you stay for a minute?" Lindsey asked him.

"Sure. Could you get me a beer?"

"I'll get it," Margo said, wanting to give them some time together.

When she returned with a cold can of beer Lindsey was saying: "I don't get it. You say you have a right to have her for a weekend every month, but then you only take her for a day. And today you brought her home an hour early."

After cracking open the beer Brandon said: "I don't know what to do with her. I mean, what do parents do with their kids?"

"They be with them," Lindsey said.

"But what do you get from being with them?"

"You get whatever you give them. But of course you have to be with them."

Brandon took a long swig of beer. "Well, I feel like she's not comfortable being with me."

"She doesn't know you. She hasn't seen you in seven years. What did you expect?"

"I don't know. I guess I didn't know what to expect."

"Did you play checkers with her?" Margo asked.

"Oh, yeah. We played five games. And she won every one of them."

"She's a bright girl. She beats me more than half the time."

"But not all the time," he said as if it really bothered him to lose to a twelve-year-old girl.

"Let me ask you," Lindsey said. "Do you like being with her?"

Brandon paused, taking another swig of beer. "I don't mind being with her. But I'd rather be with someone my own age."

"Do you have a girlfriend now?"

"Well, I did until two months ago, but I don't now."

Margo noted that he had reappeared in their lives exactly two months ago.

"If you had a girlfriend now," Lindsey said, "would you rather be with her than with your daughter?"

"I guess I would."

"So you only want to be with Keira to fill the gap between girlfriends?"

"It doesn't fill the gap," he said. "It's only one day a month. So what's your problem?"

"My problem is, I don't want Keira to build up hopes of having a father and then get dumped when you find another girlfriend."

"I wouldn't do that to her."

"You better not. So think about it."

Brandon killed his beer and then got up to leave, saying: "You know, I have to admit, I don't know how you do it."

"Do what?"

"Raise children. It's not easy."

"No, it's not. So please don't make it harder."

As she watched him walk to his car Margo hoped that Brandon had learned something from this experience.

A few minutes later Keira appeared as if she had been waiting for her father to leave, and she sat down with them.

"I heard you played checkers," Lindsey told her.

"Yeah. It wasn't much fun," Keira said. "I even tried to lose so he could win a game, and he still couldn't win."

"Maybe it's not his game," Margo said.

"Maybe. But he didn't seem to know what else to do with me."

"He didn't show you any games on your phone?"

"No. And I didn't ask him." Keira was silent, and then she said: "You know what I think?"

"What do you think?" Lindsey asked her.

"I think he's lonely. And I feel bad for him."

"I think you're right," Margo said.

"I wish I could help him," Keira said. "But I don't know how."

"I don't either," Lindsey said. "Do you want to see him next month?"

"Mm." Keria frowned. "I guess I do. But I don't want to spend the whole weekend with him. Do I have to?"

"No. You only have to spend the day with him."

"Good. I wish he was like Chavo or Anthony," Keira said plaintively. "How did I end up with him as a father?"

"That's my fault," Lindsey said.

"But if he hadn't been your father," Margo said, "you wouldn't exist. So be thankful."

Keira nodded as if she almost understood.

The next day after they got home from church she saw there was a message on her landline. It was from Lupe, whom she called right away, praying it was good news.

"They let Chavo back into the country," Lupe told her.

"Thank God," Margo said, closing her eyes.

"He called me from the airport as soon as he got through immigration. He's on his way home now."

"Please tell him how much we missed him, and ask him to call me later today, when he has a chance."

"Okay. Do you want him to go to work tomorrow?"

Margo laughed. "No, he should spend time with you and Pablo. I just want to welcome him home."

She shared the news with her family, knowing it would make them happy because they understood how much she had been worrying that the government wouldn't let Chavo back into the country. Of course it made Tricia especially happy because with Chavo back she would be relieved from working in the kitchen of the café.

Chavo called her in the middle of the afternoon. By then Tricia had gone to the restaurant, which was now open on Sundays, and Lindsey and Keira had gone to the pool. She talked with Chavo for about a half hour, bringing him up to date on things and giving him a paid vacation for the time he had spent in Mexico. She learned that his mother had died peacefully, comforted by his presence at her bedside, and she resolved to offer a Mass for her on the next available Sunday.

After ending the call she decided to have a party to celebrate Chavo's safe return, and that night after coming home from work Tricia suggested that they have the party at the restaurant. Margo liked the idea, and they scheduled it for the Sunday after Labor Day weekend. They made up a guest list that included their family, their friends, their employees, and their customers. Tricia used an online service to invite people, and she organized things, including the delivery of beer and wine, which they could serve because it was a private party.

Guests were expected to start arriving at four in the afternoon, so after church they went to the café to get things ready. Margo and Keira arranged the tables, covered them with cloths, and set them with glasses, napkins, tableware, and place cards while Tricia went into the kitchen to coordinate the food with Peter, who with the help of two assistants had been preparing a Chinese banquet. Around three thirty the waiters arrived, and Tricia set up for the cocktail hour.

By four thirty the place was packed, the adults were drinking beer and wine, and the children were drinking punch. The noise level was so high that Margo had to shout to get people's attention for what she wanted to say. When they finally quieted down she said: "As you know, we're here to celebrate the safe return of Chavo who for more than five years has been the key to the success of our café. So let's drink a toast to Chavo, and let's thank him for everything he's done for us."

Mostly in English people said "Thank you, Chavo," but a few said "*Gracias, Chavo.*"

She then invited Chavo to say a few words, and standing by her side he said: "Thank you for this party. And *gracias a Dios* for bringing me home to my family."

When it was time for food they all found the tables where they had been assigned, and they sat down. Chavo and his wife were with Lindsey, Keira, and Tricia, and Shannon and her family were with Patrick and Donna, and Greta was with Robert and four longtime customers.

The waiters went around and refilled glasses with beer, wine, and punch, and then they brought the first three courses in the banquet—walnut shrimp, long life noodles, and steamed whole fish.

Before she joined Chavo at his table Margo scanned the room, and she observed that her family, her friends, her employees, and her customers were all having a good time, and she wished that Jack could have attended. He would have enjoyed it.

After sitting down she bowed her head and prayed for Anthony, who had saved her business and made this celebration possible.

Book Club Guide to

Margo's Café

Tom Milton

Introduction

Margo Walsh, a seventy-year-old widow who lives with a daughter and a granddaughter in the house where she grew up, is struggling to pay property taxes that keep increasing because people with a lot of money are moving to her village from the city and bidding up prices of homes. With the influx of these people, who seem to have no limits on their spending, the village is becoming unaffordable for working-class people. Margo, who lives mainly on Social Security, has been able to supplement her income with what she earns from a café that she started five years ago. Her café is open from eight in the morning to three in the afternoon offering takeout, breakfast, and lunch, and until now its profits have helped pay her property taxes. But her new landlord, an investor from the city, is doubling her rent, so she faces the risk of losing her business and being forced to sell her house. Of course her house has risen in value, but she would have to share the proceeds of a sale with her siblings, so she wouldn't get enough money to buy or rent an apartment with the space she needs for her family in the area where she has lived her whole life. To save her house she must either find a job, which will be difficult for a woman her age, or expand her business by offering dinner in the evening, which will be risky. And while she is struggling to survive she must deal with the problems of her children and her grandchildren.

Her key employee at the café is a young man named Chavo who runs the kitchen cooking breakfast and lunch, and preparing dinners for customers to take home and warm up in the evening. Like most of the people working in kitchens he's an immigrant, but since he was only a child of five when his parents illegally brought him here from Mexico he has a special status in which he might have a chance of becoming legal someday and is temporarily not at risk of being deported. Chavo is in his late twenties, married to a young woman with the same status who delivered a baby boy about three months ago. They live in an apartment in South Yonkers which they can afford only because Chavo has a job at the café in addition to his main job at an Italian restaurant in a nearby village. Margo would like to engage him as a partner in expanding her business, but if he quit his main job to offer dinner at the café he would be at risk if the venture failed, and she doesn't want to expose him to such a risk. But if she closes the café he will have to find another second job, which might not be easy because restaurants still haven't fully recovered from covid.

The daughter living with Margo is her middle child, Lindsey, who has a job as a mental health worker at a private hospital that treats children with serious psychiatric issues. Lindsey has a bachelor's degree in psychology, and she was working on a master's degree when she got pregnant accidentally. As soon as her father, Jack, found out about it he forced her boyfriend to marry her, and the marriage lasted almost six years, but after enduring his drug addictions and repeated infidelities she finally divorced him, and now at the age of thirty-six, with a twelve-year-old daughter, she has given up the idea of getting a master's degree, so she's stuck in a low-paying job, working the day shift from eight to four, though that's an improvement over her schedules before she had seniority. Lindsey contributes to the expenses of Margo's house, but with her low salary she could never afford to rent an apartment in the area where they live, and if they had to move somewhere else her daughter, Keira, would be uprooted from her school and her friends.

Keira is a bright girl but is easily influenced by social media, which has gotten her into trouble. After the last such incident Margo stopped leaving Keira alone in the house even for a minute, so she is always there when Keira gets home from school, and she keeps the girl occupied until her mother gets home from work. This schedule works for Margo because she works at her café from eight in the morning to three in the afternoon, when she closes it. But if she expands her business by offering dinner she won't be able to maintain that schedule unless she finds a partner for her business. So she decides to look for a partner, and to get some advice she meets with her eldest daughter, Shannon, who manages a senior complex that includes facilities for independent living, assisted living, and a nursing home. After some discussion Shannon suggests that Margo might be able to find a job managing a restaurant based on her experience in managing the café, and she also explains how Margo can use the internet not only to find such a job but also to find a partner.

At this point her life is disrupted further by her youngest daughter, Tricia, who dropped out of college after one semester and works as a bartender, changing jobs and changing boyfriends repeatedly. As soon as she has saved enough money she quits her job and goes on a trip with her boyfriend, and then returns and breaks up with the boyfriend and finds another job. Her latest boyfriend is a suave young man who claims to belong to an old, wealthy Mexican family, but Margo doesn't trust him, and she is upset when she learns that Tricia has quit her latest job and is going to Mexico with him. So she is worried about Tricia being in Mexico, which based on what she hears on the news is rife with kidnappings and gang violence.

Following Shannon's advice she pursues her search for a job or a partner, but she doesn't find either, and she has begun to lose hope when a young man named Anthony Chen comes into her café and gives her an idea on how to expand her business. Seeing no other possibilities, she bets her life on his idea.

A conversation with Tom Milton

In this novel, instead of telling the story about a protagonist with a mission to oppose some injustice in the world, you tell the story about an elderly widow struggling to survive in a changing world while dealing with the problems of her children and her grandchildren. What made you want to tell this story?

Because I see it everywhere. Like many mothers these days, Margo never gets a rest from dealing with the problems of her children and her grandchildren. During the summer she can sit on the front porch of her house in the evening and try to relax after a long day of work, but she always has to worry about her family.

That's why she wants to stay in her house—it's for her family. Two of her children still live with her, as well as one of her grandchildren. If she was living alone, she'd have more options.

She would, but for an elderly woman living alone isn't a great option. I mean, imagine her living alone in a studio apartment far from the village where she grew up and has lived her whole life. That would sad.

So with two children and a grandchild living with her, still needing her, she has a meaningful role in life.

When you and I were growing up, we were expected to leave home and live on our own and be independent. But things have changed. Among the elderly people I know almost all of them have children who to some extent are dependent on them, and in some cases still live with them.

Well, one reason is that housing is so expensive now in relation to what young people earn. When I got out of college I could rent a one-bedroom apartment in Manhattan on a salary that wouldn't pay for my car insurance now.

Children could leave home then, and their parents could remain in their homes without the heavy burden of property taxes. Now, more people are living in extended families for financial reasons.

But wasn't it always that way?

It was until a period after World War II that lasted maybe thirty or forty years. But that was an exceptional period.

So getting back to your main theme—the role of a mother protecting her children from the evils of this world. That role hasn't changed, has it?

Well, there have always been evils in this world, but in recent years their effects have been amplified by technology.

You mean by social media.

Yes. Social media are a conduit for the evil spirits who prowl about the world seeking the ruin of children.

That's from the prayer to St. Michael the Archangel.

Right. And we hope he'll protect children against social media, but mothers are the first line of defense.

So this novel isn't just about a woman struggling to save her business or her house, it's about a mother struggling to protect her children and her grandchildren from the evils of this world.

A mother struggling against a world ruled by the love of money, which uses social media to achieve its goals.

You addressed this issue in The Godmother *where an adopted girl is lured by social media into a dangerous search for her birth mother.*

There are so many ways that social media can harm children. When Keira's biological father exposes her to an online game that promotes violence, both her mother and her grandmother intervene to protect her. Those games are designed to be addictive, just like everything on social media. They addict children to get information, and they make money selling that information to advertisers. It's an evil exploitation of children.

Even Margo's oldest daughter, who has provided a stable loving home for her children, encounters this evil.

It can happen to anyone's children.

I liked her reaction to what social media did to her daughter.

I wish more people would react like that. The problem is that the social media companies fend off efforts to stop them by invoking the right to free speech. It's like the promoters of guns invoking the Second Amendment, which was originally intended to protect our freedom but instead is being used to expose our children to gun violence.

You addressed that issue in Voices in Ramah *where your protagonist, who lost her daughter in a school shooting, pursues the mission of banning assault weapons.*

I wish we could make some progress on that.

In this novel you also raise the issue of drugs, which you addressed in The Lineman *and* A Residue of Hope.

Margo's youngest daughter was almost killed because of her relationship with a man who she didn't know was a drug dealer, and her middle daughter divorced her husband, the father of her child, because he was addicted to drugs. So many people are affected by drugs that it's hard to write a realistic novel set at the present time without encountering the drug issue.

And then there's the issue of immigration.

Margo's chef, on whom she depends for her café, is a young man who through no fault of his own was brought to this country by his parents illegally when he was five, and for reasons that are purely political he's living in jeopardy while working and raising a family and contributing to this country.

I thought they passed a law to protect people in his situation.

They proposed such a law, but Congress never passed it. So when Chavo wants to visit his mother on her deathbed in Mexico he must take the risk that our government won't let him back into this country.

Well, at least the situation of Anthony isn't the fault of our government.

No, it's the fault of a government that simply can't tolerate human rights. But if we don't want to end up with a government like that, then we can't be complacent. We must resist people who push us in that direction.

A final thought. It struck me that while Margo struggles to survive and deal with the problems of her children and her grandchildren, she's usually in a situation where she has no control. Like when her new landlord doubles the rent for her café, or when the local governments increase the property taxes on her home, or when her youngest daughter gets wounded by a gunshot, or when the chef of her café may be not allowed to return from a visit to his dying mother in Mexico, or when her grandchildren become victims of social media. Though Margo is a capable, resourceful woman she usually faces challenges where all she can do is hope and pray. Are you suggesting that we all live in that kind of world?

Ultimately, we all live in that kind of world. So hoping and praying, I believe, is the right response.

Well, thanks for giving us another great novel about real people in real situations today.

You're welcome. And thanks for another great conversation.

Discussion questions

1. What is this novel mainly about?

2. What personal qualities does Margo have that enable her to survive in a changing world?

3. How does her friend Greta complement her?

4. Do you think Margo deals effectively with the problems of her children and her grandchildren?

5. Discuss how Keira and Patty are affected by social media.

6. Do you think the interventions by Margo, Lindsey, and Shannon to protect them from social media will be effective?

7. What kind of growth do you see in the character of Tricia? In the character of Lindsey?

8. What do you think of the way Lindsey handles the efforts of her ex-husband to spend his entitled time with his daughter?

9. How do you think Keira will deal with this situation?

10. Explain why you agree or disagree with Margo's decision not to ask Chavo to be her partner.

11. How does the author address the issue of immigration with the role given to Chavo in the story?

12. What does Margo see in Anthony that makes her trust him?

13. What kind of future do you envision for Anthony?